"You were leaving." His voice was soft, his tone not dismayed or disappointed, but disillusioned. *"Without saying goodbye. And you weren't coming back."*

And finally she had no choice but to face him. The lie was there, ready to come out—*I needed a break. Just a few days. Charleston or Savannah or Beaufort. I would have been back* ███ ██ ██ *week.* But all she did was nod.

It was as if someth██████ ████████ █████████nced on her, backing ████████ █████ ████████ █ mere inches from hers, ██████ ██████ ██ on either side of her head, h██ ████ ██ hers. "Why?" he demanded, the que████ ██ ██ the more fierce for its low, insistent tone. "Because of Martha? Who was she, Ellie? What did she want from you? Where were you going? What about us?"

She took a breath, shallow and painful, and whispered, "There is no 'us.'"

Dear Reader,

When Detective Tommy Maricci made his first appearance in Copper Lake, I knew immediately that he would be a future hero. Who could resist a tall, dark and sexy Italian-American cop? Not me. I married one. (Though deli owner Ellie Chase tries her best. Otherwise, there'd be no story.)

Having a cop in the family comes in really handy when you're writing romantic suspense. I'm the rare author who doesn't like interviewing sources for my books, so my husband handles all that for me. If he doesn't know the answer to a particular question in any aspect of law enforcement or the justice system, one of his buddies does. Another plus: his years with the police department and the Naval Criminal Investigation Service have given him excellent investigative and interrogation skills, so he can also get the answers for all my non-cop questions, too. A resource, a researcher and my own hero all rolled into one. What more could I ask for?

Hope you enjoy this visit with my *second*-favorite Italian-American cop.

Marilyn

MARILYN PAPPANO

Passion to Die For

Silhouette®

Romantic

SUSPENSE

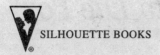

SILHOUETTE BOOKS

Recycling programs
for this product may
not exist in your area.

ISBN-13: 978-0-373-27649-3

PASSION TO DIE FOR

Visit Silhouette Books at www.eHarlequin.com

Printed in U.S.A.

Books by Marilyn Pappano

Silhouette Romantic Suspense

MARILYN PAPPANO

has spent most of her life growing into the person she was meant to be, but isn't there yet. She's been blessed by family—her husband, their son, his lovely wife and a grandson who is almost certainly the most beautiful and talented baby in the world—and friends, along with a writing career that's made her one of the luckiest people around. Her passions, besides those already listed, include the pack of wild dogs who make their home in her house, fighting the good fight against the weeds that make up her yard, killing the creepy-crawlies that slither out of those weeds and, of course, anything having to do with books.

Chapter 1

Ellie Chase loved her job. Owning a restaurant had long been a dream of hers, way back in the times when she didn't have many dreams, when she was sleeping on the street or scrounging for a meal. She'd savored sweet visions of a diner, a café, a bistro, warm when it was cold, dry when it rained, safe and welcoming and, of course, filled with all the good food her sixteen-year-old belly had ached for.

Tonight, though, she'd rather be working nine to five at some dreary job where all the responsibilities fell on someone else's shoulders.

She was seated on a stool at the end of their newly installed bar, receipts, schedules and a glass of iced tea in front of her. Outside it was pouring rain, and the temperature was about twenty degrees colder than normal for October in east-central Georgia. In spite of the weather, business had been good—if you counted running out of broccoli cheese soup, fresh bread and banana cheesecake as good. The oven was being temperamental again, and so was Dharma, her self-proclaimed chef. One of the waitresses had called in sick, a customer had mumbled something about a problem in the men's bathroom and Tommy Maricci had come in for dinner.

With a date.

To top it all off, her feet were aching, her head was throbbing and though it was nearly closing time, no one besides her and her staff showed any interest in going home.

Carmen, her best waitress and unofficial assistant manager, slid onto the stool next to her. "You want me to comp Russ and Jamie for their dinner?"

"Yes, please." Russ Calloway, owner of Copper Lake's biggest construction company, had fixed the overflowing toilet in the men's room, saving her from putting in a call to her overpriced and very-difficult-to-reach plumber. She was grateful, even if he had come in with Tommy and his date.

"I want you to know, I didn't step on Sophy's toes, spill her drink on her or spit in her food, even though I was tempted."

Ellie managed only half a smile. "Sophy's nice."

"I know, and if I worked for her over in the quilt shop instead of here, I'd be hating you. But I don't. The least he could do is take his dates somewhere else."

"His money is as good as anyone else's. Besides, I'm so over him that I don't care."

Carmen gave her a long look, from the top of her head to the pointed toes of her favorite black heels. *Tommy's favorite,* the devil residing on her shoulder whispered. They made her legs look a mile long and showed her butt to good advantage— Amanda Calloway, retired exotic dancer, had taught her that— and they drew the sweetest, naughtiest little grin from Tommy every time he saw her wearing them.

At least, they used to.

"Uh-huh," Carmen drawled at last. "I can tell from the way you're hiding in here instead of working out front like you always do. And from all those dates you've been accepting."

"Hey, your social life is active enough for both of us."

Carmen snorted. "I'm married, honey. My social life consists of work, church, taxiing the kids around and trying to schedule sex with my husband at least once a month."

"You've got five kids. See how well you're succeeding?" Ellie hadn't had sex since last April. She'd thought it was make-up sex—her relationship with Tommy had always been an on-again, off-again thing. When it was over, he'd put on his clothes, kissed her, said he was sorry and walked out. She'd known it would happen someday—people always gave up on her eventually—but not that day. It had hurt more than it was supposed to.

But she was over it now.

And if she told the lie often enough, she might even believe it.

With a grunt, Carmen slid to her feet. "Let me start politely hurrying these people along. They need to get home where they belong so we can do the same."

Ellie's house on Cypress Creek Road was pretty, cozy, had two bedrooms and was even emptier than her life. It was the place where she stayed, but it wasn't home. She didn't belong there. She'd never really belonged anywhere besides the restaurant.

But it was more than she'd ever expected to have. She wouldn't whine about the things that were missing.

She'd just gotten back to work when Gina, one of the part-time waitresses, approached. "Hey, Ellie, there's a woman out front who wants to talk to you."

"An unhappy customer?" she asked warily. Her food was first-rate and the service even better, but some people always found something to complain about. She comped more meals than anyone could reasonably expect in the name of customer satisfaction.

"Nope. Never seen her before. I told her I'd bring her back here, but she said no, she would wait on the porch."

Great. In the cold. At least the awning Ellie had installed over the summer would keep her dry. Still, she swung by the office to grab her coat before she skirted through the main dining room to the front door. Unwillingly her gaze strayed to the three tables pushed together in the center of the room, where Tommy Maricci and Sophy Marchand were sitting with Russ and Robbie Calloway and their wives. Their dessert plates were empty, and they were making the restless movements Ellie associated with saying goodbyes.

Tommy would take Sophy home, of course, even though the house that held her shop on the first floor and her apartment on the second was just across the square and around the corner. He would escort her inside; maybe because he was a cop, maybe because his father had raised him right, he was big on that sort of thing. Would he spend the night? Was he sleeping with her?

She didn't care. She was over him.

A blast of cold hit when she opened the door. A woman waited in the shadows at the end of the porch, her back to Ellie, the hood of her trench coat pulled over her head.

Ellie shrugged into her own coat, belting the wool around her waist, uncuffing the sleeves so they covered most of her fingers. Stopping a few feet from the woman, she said, "Hi. I'm Ellie Chase. I understand you want to talk to me."

"Ellie. Is that short for something?"

The voice was low, hoarse, probably from years of smoking. Even with the breeze and the fresh scent of rain, Ellie could smell stale cigarette smoke, as if it permeated the woman so thoroughly that it had no choice but to leach into the air surrounding her.

"Ellen," she said impatiently. "Can I help you with something?"

"Ellen. Hmm. You sure? You don't look like an Ellen. In fact, you look like…oh, a Bethany to me."

Wind gusted along the length of the porch. That was the reason Ellie felt so cold inside, why she felt as if her knees might give out. She staggered a step before gripping the back of the nearest chair, her fingers knotting so tightly around the cold wood that they went instantly numb.

"I'm sure," she said, her voice sounding flat and cold. "I know my own name."

Slowly the woman turned. The hood cast shadows over the upper half of her face, leaving only an impression in the dim light of aged skin, deep grooves, an overglossed mouth. "So do I," she said. "I know the name you use now, and I know the name you were born to. Bethany Ann Dempsey."

She raised one weathered hand to pull the hood back, and Ellie stared. Her stomach knotted, and tremors shot through her, making her shiver uncontrollably inside her coat. It had been fifteen years since she'd last seen the woman, and time hadn't been kind. Her hair was a dull, lifeless gray, her skin sallow. Too much tobacco, too much booze and too damn much meanness had combined to add an additional fifteen years to her face. The only thing that remained the same as in Ellie's memories was her eyes. Blue. Cold. Cruel.

"What's the matter, Beth?" The woman smiled, and that, too, was the same: smug and vicious. "Surprised to see your mama?"

For a moment, a dull haze surrounded Ellie, blocking out sound, cold, rain and wind. Anger, loss and panic welled inside her, each fighting for control, the anger curling her fingers into fists, the panic urging her to run, run *right now*. That terrified little girl would have run, but she was gone. The woman she'd become wouldn't give in to emotion.

"As far as I'm concerned, my mother died fifteen years ago."
Shoulders back, Ellie turned and took a few steps toward the
door before Martha Dempsey spoke again.

"You've made a place for yourself here, haven't you? Nice
restaurant. Nice little blue house. You go to church. You're a
member of the Copper Lake Merchants' Association. You rub
elbows with the rich folks in town. People think you're something, don't they? But they don't know what I know."

Ellie hovered, frozen in the act of taking a step. After a
quavery moment, her foot touched the floor and she pivoted to
face Martha, freezing again when the screen door creaked open.
Jamie and Russ Calloway came out first, not noticing her,
heading directly for the steps. Behind them were Robbie
Calloway and Sophy Marchand, lost in conversation, and
bringing up the rear were Robbie's wife, Anamaria, and Tommy.

Half wishing to remain unseen, Ellie knew it wasn't going
to happen. Anamaria was her closest friend in town, and she
was sensitive to emotions, conflicts and auras. Her gaze came
immediately to Ellie's, her dark eyes taking in what was
probably a fireworks display of auras.

Moving gracefully despite her pregnancy, Anamaria closed
the distance between them, smiled at Martha, then wrapped one
arm around Ellie. "Dinner was wonderful, as usual, Ellie."
Leaning closer, her mouth brushing Ellie's ear, she murmured,
"If you need me…"

"Thanks." Ellie squeezed her hand more tightly than she'd
intended, too aware that Tommy was waiting, a distinct look of
suspicion on his face. All the other times they'd broken up, they'd
remained friends, but this time he never smiled at her and never
spoke if he could avoid it. This time he'd said it was for good, and
though she'd denied it for the first month, finally she believed him.

When Anamaria went back to him at the top of the steps, he
was still wearing that look. His gaze met hers for an instant,

but he didn't acknowledge her. Instead, he broke contact, took Anamaria's arm and escorted her down the wet steps.

"Does *she* know?" Martha asked, her tone sly and taunting. "Do they?"

People believed she had no family, that her parents were dead and all that was left were distant cousins. They thought she'd been raised in Charleston, where she had, in fact, done a fair amount of growing up, that she'd lived a normal, if somewhat family-deficient, life.

Ironically, Anamaria, whom she'd known the shortest time, had guessed there was more to Ellie than the story she told. But that was none of Martha's business. Nothing about Ellie was her business.

"How did you find me?"

Martha grinned and lifted one bony shoulder in a shrug. "I've got my sources."

"What do you want?"

Martha felt in her pockets, coming up with a pack of cigarettes and a cheap lighter. Ellie let her shake one out and slide it between her lips, then said, "Don't smoke here."

Martha hesitated, hands cupped to protect the lighter's flame, then slowly lowered it. She left the cigarette in her mouth, though. For forty years she'd talked around one. Lit or unlit didn't matter. "Your father died four months ago."

No surprise. No disappointment. No regret. The news meant nothing to Ellie, and that was a sad thing.

"Nothing to keep me in Atlanta anymore."

Oliver Dempsey may not have amounted to anything as a father, but he'd brought home a steady paycheck, enough to cover the basics: housing, transportation, food, booze, tobacco. He'd resented spending any of that paycheck on a teenage daughter whom he considered pretty much worthless, but he'd taken good care of himself and Martha.

And now she wanted someone else to take care of her.

Ellie wanted to laugh, but was afraid what kind of sound would squeeze through the tightness in her throat. "You want money. From me. Is that it?"

Martha stiffened defensively. "I am your mother."

"Like hell you are. You gave birth to me, you changed a few diapers and you fed me until I was old enough to feed myself. That doesn't make you my mother."

"Don't you get smart with me—"

"Remember the last time I saw you?" Ellie interrupted. "When I pleaded with you to let me come home? When I was hungry and sleeping in abandoned buildings and I *begged* you to help me?"

Martha's expression was contempt tinged with regret. Not because she regretted throwing her teenage daughter out of the house, not because she'd never loved or protected Ellie the way a mother was supposed to, but because her past actions were going to interfere with getting what she wanted now. She was about to be held accountable, and Martha had always hated being accountable.

"You had to learn a lesson," she said sourly.

"What lesson? That I couldn't count on my parents? I already knew that. That the next carton of cigarettes and the next case of beer were more important to you than me? I knew that, too. Just what the hell lesson was I supposed to be learning out there?"

"Don't you cuss at me. I didn't tolerate it back then, and I won't now. You won't disrespect me."

The urge to laugh bubbled inside Ellie. The idea that she felt anything remotely resembling respect for this woman was ludicrous. If Martha dropped dead in front of her right that moment, she would feel nothing more than relief that such an ugly part of her life had ended.

"You want money," Ellie said again, her voice flat. "How much?"

Martha smiled, showing teeth in need of care and greed that made her eyes damn near sparkle. "Well, now, it's hard to say. Like I said, your daddy's dead. There's no reason for me to stay in Atlanta, and truth is, it's a little late in life for me to be starting a new career. I kind of like the idea of retiring, resettling to be close to my girl and the grandbabies she's sure to give me someday. I looked around that pretty little house of yours, and that back bedroom would suit me fine. I could even help out down here sometimes, you know, welcome customers to our restaurant and chat with them about this and that."

Ellie's spine was stiff enough to hurt. There was no way she would ever let Martha move into her house or help out at her restaurant. She'd burn both places down before letting Martha taint them. Drawing on the cold deep inside her, she said, "So you get a better life than you've ever known. And what do I get in return?"

Martha's vicious smile reappeared. "Your fancy friends don't find out about this." From under the trench coat, she produced a manila envelope. "Here. You can keep it. It's just copies."

When Ellie made no move to touch it, Martha tossed the envelope on the seat of the rocker next to her, then tugged her coat tighter. "I don't expect you to say yes right now. Take a walk down Memory Lane. Think about what you stand to lose. I'll be in touch with you in a day or two."

Ellie numbly watched her pull the hood over her limp hair, then clump past and down the steps into the rain. She didn't look to see which way Martha went. The only place Ellie wanted her to go was away, and that wasn't going to happen until she had what she wanted.

When everything was still, Ellie picked up the envelope with unwilling fingers and hid it inside her own coat. She would take that stroll down Memory Lane—more like Nightmare Street—later. First, she had a restaurant to close for the night.

The clock in the hall chimed eleven times, rousing Tommy from the edges of sleep. The television was still on, framed between his booted feet propped on the coffee table, and Sophy was snuggled beside him, her sweater rustling against his shirt as she shifted. Damn, he must have fallen asleep not long after they'd settled on the couch.

"I should go home."

"Or you could spend the night."

He could. It wasn't as if he had someone to go home to. And he'd slept over before—not a lot but enough to be comfortable with the idea. But having dinner at Ellie's Deli had guaranteed that his mind would be on someone else—looking for glimpses of her, waiting for her to come to the table to greet them like the old friends they were, wondering how he'd been lucky enough to go there on a day when she wore his favorite outfit: white blouse with a deep V and black skirt that clung to her hips so snugly that it needed a slit so she could walk. Conservative clothes that concealed a tiny lace bra and matching thong, all set off by those incredible black heels. Just the sight of them...

His body twitched, and he silently cursed, hoping Sophy hadn't noticed. He wouldn't insult her by pretending he wanted her when Ellie was all over his mind. Her sleek blond hair. Her amazing legs. The confident way she moved. Her smiles, ranging from polite to intimate to wicked.

Oh, yeah, and the drop-dead cold shoulder she gave him these days.

"When it takes you that long to come up with an answer, it's pretty clear." Sophy sat up, lowering her feet to the floor.

An answer to...? Then he remembered: staying the night.

"I'm sorry, babe. It's just…I've got to work tomorrow, and it's been a long day—"

"And spending the evening at Ellie's wasn't the best way to get in the mood to sleep with another woman." Sophy scooted to the edge of the couch, then looked at him. "Can I ask you something?"

"Sure."

"Rumor is that you broke up with her. If she's got this much effect on you six months later, why'd you do it?"

He'd issued an ultimatum, and then he'd had to live with it. He'd demanded marriage, kids, living together, commitment and she'd opted for nothing. It had been a lonely six months, but faced with the same situation, he'd make the same demand. He wanted more than a long-term girlfriend. If she couldn't give him that, someone else could.

Like Sophy.

"It's complicated," he said, getting to his feet and pulling her with him. Keeping hold of her hand, he went to the front door, where he snagged his jacket from the coat tree. After sliding it on, he wrapped his arms around Sophy and kissed her.

She tilted her head so the kiss fell on her cheek. "Are you still in love with her?"

Grimly he gave the best answer he could. "I'm trying not to be."

Sophy studied him for a moment, then leaned forward and brushed her mouth across his. "You're still welcome to spend the night. I know, not tonight. But maybe next time."

"Sure." Provided they didn't go to the deli, and he didn't see or think about Ellie all night. Yeah, then he might be good for someone else.

"It's all right about her," Sophy said. "I mean, I knew going in…"

Somehow that didn't make him feel better. He said goodbye

and brushed a kiss across her forehead, then opened the door
to a blast of cold air. Closing it quickly behind him, he took the
wooden steps two at a time, shoved his hands in his jacket
pockets and set off down the street.

It had been Sophy's suggestion that they walk home from
dinner. Between the canopies that covered the storefronts and the
live oaks that shielded the path through the square, they'd arrived
significantly drier than if they'd walked the block north with no
cover to his SUV. Now, with everything closed up for the night
and the streets empty, he wished for a closer parking space.

Tommy was passing the gazebo in the square when a rustle
of movement caught his attention. Someone hunkered on one
of the benches inside the structure. The dark coat could belong
to anyone; the pale blond hair could only be Ellie's. What the
hell was she doing there?

He wanted to walk on. He should have, but he was a cop.
He didn't like things out of place, and Ellie alone in the square
late at night was definitely out of place. She should have finished closing up the restaurant over an hour ago, should have
been home in bed.

Should have been home in bed with him.

When his boot landed on the first step, she stiffened, then
whirled around to face him. There was a moment of surprise on
her face, then that blankness he'd come to associate with her. She
sat straighter, pulled her coat tighter and something papery rustled.

He stopped halfway up the steps, on eye level with her, and
allowed himself a moment to just look at her. Light blond hair
falling past her chin, sleek and elegant like her. Skin the color
of warm, dark honey. Brown eyes, a surprise on first sight,
damned sexy every other time. She was shorter than his five feet
eleven inches, slender, with great breasts and hips, but always
lamenting that she enjoyed her own food too much.

He'd never agreed. Not from the very first time he'd seen

her and thought *damn*. Damn, she was beautiful. Damn, she was hot. Damn, he was lost. Five years he'd been lost, and he'd hoped to stay that way forever.

His hands clenched inside his pockets. "You okay?"

"Of course."

Of course. During all the rough patches they'd gone through, she'd never cried, pouted or moped. She'd never pleaded with him or shown a moment's weakness. She'd always been stronger, less affected, than he. He admired her strength, but would it have killed her to need him even half as much as he'd needed her?

"What are you doing out here?"

"Enjoying the lovely evening. What are you doing?"

"I was at Sophy's."

If that news bothered her, she didn't let it show. Was she the least bit jealous? He wished. Did she miss him? Maybe. Would she ever marry him? Doubtful. If she hadn't loved him enough after five years, why should a sixth or eighth or tenth year make a difference?

"How is Sophy?" she asked.

"You could have come to the table and seen for yourself this evening." He'd waited through the appetizers and the salads for her to do just that. By the time the main course had arrived, he'd accepted that she wasn't going to.

"I was busy."

"You're always busy. Running things. Talking to customers." Was it a good thing that she'd avoided his table? Had she not wanted to acknowledge him with Sophy?

He took another step up. "I saw you talking to that woman on the porch." Stupid comment. Of course he'd seen them and she knew it; he'd passed within a few feet of them. "I didn't recognize her."

The thin light from the streetlamps showed her shrug, stiff and awkward. "She doesn't live here."

"An old friend?"

"No."

"A relative?"

She was stiffer, more awkward. "Just someone who wanted something."

He thought back to the woman. If asked, he would have said he hadn't really paid much attention to her; he'd been too busy not paying attention to Ellie. But he'd seen enough. The woman had looked to be in her sixties, average height and weight. Gray hair, sallow complexion, a heavy smoker and on edge. Even when standing still, she hadn't been still. Shifting her weight, her gaze darting about, her attention honed.

What had she wanted from Ellie? A handout? A favor? And why Ellie?

Because they shared a connection somewhere in their past? In the five years Ellie had lived in Copper Lake, she'd had little to say about her twenty-five years elsewhere. She was an only child, her parents were dead, and her only relatives were distant, figuratively and literally. He knew she'd had some unhappy times, but she'd never been open to discussing them.

A woman should be willing to discuss her hurts and disappointments with the man she'd been seeing for the better part of five years.

The wind gusted, scattering sodden dead leaves across the square, and it sent a chill through him. His jeans and leather jacket weren't enough to stand up to the cold, but Ellie didn't seem to notice the temperature. Granted, she wore a long wool coat, but there was an air of detachment about her. Anamaria would probably say her aura was the translucent shade of blue ice.

"Why don't you go home?" he suggested, wanting very much to do the same.

"Are you going to continue harassing me if I don't, Detective?"

"Come on, Ellie." He wasn't comfortable leaving her, or any

other woman, alone in the gazebo with midnight approaching. Copper Lake's crime rate was nothing compared to the big cities, but bad things still happened to innocent people.

She opened her mouth as if to argue, then closed it again and stood, arms still folded across her middle. There was another papery crackle. From something hidden beneath her coat?

She passed without touching him, and when he fell into step beside her, she scowled. "I can make it to my car alone."

"It's on my way."

Those were the last words either of them said until they reached the small parking lot that opened off the alley behind the deli. Her lime-green VW Beetle was the only car in the lot, parked under the lone streetlight, its lights flashing when she clicked the remote. She would have gotten in and driven away without a word, but he laid his hand on her arm, stopping her.

"Ellie, if you need to talk—"

Even through the bulk of the coat, he felt her muscles clench. She looked at him, then at his hand, and he withdrew it. The night chill had nothing on her gaze. "Thank you for the escort."

Her polite words were as bogus as his response. "You're welcome." Pushing his hand into his pocket, Tommy stepped back and watched as she slid behind the wheel, started the engine, then drove away. He stood motionless long after her taillights disappeared down the alley, until another blast of wind hit him, this time dampened with more rain moving in.

Damn, she was cold. Damn, she was distant.

And damned if he didn't still love her.

Ellie's house was located at the end of Cypress Creek Road, just before it made a sharp right turn and became Magnolia Drive. It wasn't a trendy part of town; her neighbors were mostly as old as her house, on the downhill side of sixty. The house was small, but the floors were hardwood, it had an attached garage and the price had been reasonable. Besides, most of her waking hours were spent at the restaurant. The house was used mostly for sleeping and doing laundry.

And, off and on until last spring, for having great sex with Tommy.

She would have been touched by his stopping at the gazebo and walking her to her car if she didn't know him so well. He would have stopped for anyone, ex-lover, acquaintance or total stranger. He was a protector from the inside out. Ensuring other people's safety wasn't just his job; it was who he *was*.

She'd desperately needed someone like that fifteen years ago. She hadn't had him then, and she couldn't have him now. Didn't deserve him now.

She let herself into the house from the garage, leaving her coat in the utility room and walking through the dimly lit kitchen into the living room. None of the furniture was anything special, and the dishes and linens had been chosen by an accommodating clerk at the housewares shop at the mall. Ellie could walk away from it all and never miss a thing.

Except, possibly, the four-inch heels she admired before kicking them off her feet.

Once she was settled comfortably on the couch, she reached for the large envelope Martha had given her, sure what was inside before she opened it. Police reports, complaints, convictions, photographs. It hurt to see herself at fifteen—still young and naive—and then at sixteen and seventeen. Like Martha, she had aged far more than the months could account for. By the age of eighteen, there'd been a hollowness about her, in her face and her eyes and her soul. She'd wanted to end it all—the pain, the shame. She'd had only one reason to live, and even that had been short-term.

Ellie went to the fireplace, put a sheet of paper on the grate and struck a match to it. As the edges curled with flame, she added another page, then another, report after photo after complaint. When the last piece was burning, she held the envelope over it, feeling the heat from the fire, holding it until she risked a burn. It dropped to the ashes on the grate, and the flames consumed it with a final wisp of smoke and a lingering, sooty fragrance. She stirred the ashes with the fireplace poker, breaking them into smaller pieces that fell through the grate, grinding them to powder until she was satisfied they'd been destroyed.

All those years ago, she hadn't thought she would live to see thirty. And here she was, not only alive but reasonably well. She had a house and a business. She had the friendship and respect of the people she did business with. She was a success by anyone's standards.

Would she still be a success if she refused Martha's blackmail?

She wanted to believe the answer was yes, that her friends would remain her friends, that who she'd become would be more important to them than who she'd been. She wanted to believe that she was good enough, changed enough, to rise above her past.

She wanted to believe that she'd earned the life she had now, that she *deserved* it.

But the truth was, she didn't know. She was a fraud, masquerading as someone no different from anyone else in Copper Lake. She'd lied to them about her background and her family. Ellie Chase was someone they could relate to. Bethany Dempsey wasn't.

She was no stranger to disappointment and rejection. Her mother and father hadn't been the first to turn away from her, nor had they been the last. And if her own parents hadn't been able to accept and forgive her, how could she count on people like the Calloways to do so?

How could she ever expect Tommy—the protector, the cop, the good guy—to do so?

She could leave. Disappear. Put the restaurant and house up for sale. Only her lawyer would need to know how to contact her, and Jamie Munroe-Calloway wouldn't share that information with anyone, especially Martha.

Let the mother who'd abandoned her bleed her dry, give up everything that mattered and run away like a coward, or stand up to Martha and risk the loss of everything—and everyone— that mattered.

It was a hell of a choice.

Chapter 2

"I hate rain."

Tommy leaned his head against the Charger's headrest and watched the house down the street through slitted eyes. He was partnered with Katherine Isaacs this week and wondering whether it was because he was good at what he did or if the lieutenant was punishing him for something.

Kiki might be the department's newest detective, but she was also its biggest whiner. She bitched about everything: rain, sun, heat, cold, driving, not driving, having to arrest someone, not getting to arrest someone.

"Piss off, Kiki," he muttered, shifting in the seat.

She scowled at him. "I hate that nickname."

"Yeah, yeah. Whine to someone who cares." It was warm inside the car, so he switched the engine on long enough to crack the windows an inch or two. Fresh air blew in, the raindrops it carried a small price to pay for its cooling effect. They'd been parked under the trees down the road from a drug dealer's house for hours now, the black Dodge practically disappearing in the gloomy overcast, and so far they hadn't seen anything more interesting than a dog taking a leak on the dealer's steps.

"Are you always this pleasant on surveillance?"

"Yeah, pretty much."

"You're supposed to be teaching me."

She stabbed at the button to roll up the window, but he'd turned off the car again. The rain wasn't coming in on her side, but the humidity was. Before long, her hair would frizz out like a '70s Afro. He knew, because she'd whined about it the first time he'd rolled down the windows.

Sprawled in the driver's seat, head tilted back, he said, "Okay, listen up. This is me teaching. When you do surveillance, you park someplace where you're not real noticeable, you settle in and you watch your target. If you're real lucky, you'll actually see something. Most of the time, you sit until your butt goes numb and you get nada. You don't eat anything that smells offensive. You don't get crumbs or wrappers in my car. You don't drink more than your bladder will hold. You don't fall asleep. And you don't complain." He turned his head so he could see her. "Oh, wait, I forgot who I was talking to. Kiki Isaacs, queen of complainers."

"That's Detective Queen of Complainers to you." She fluffed her brown hair, starting its inevitable frizz. "I don't complain. I make my opinions known. Keeping things inside is bad for your health."

"Then you must be the healthiest person I've ever met. Be quiet now. You're fogging up my windows." He used a napkin to wipe the windshield, then leaned back again.

The house they were watching sat isolated from its neighbors. A fire had taken out the house to the west, and the one to the east had been leveled by a tornado. That probably suited

Steve Terrell just fine. His own lot was overgrown, and junk filled the yard. The screens on the windows were torn and rusted, patches of shingles were missing from the roof and the paint was a truly ugly shade of purple.

An informant had told them that Terrell was expecting a shipment around nine that morning, but it was now one in the afternoon and there hadn't been any movement on the street at all. Even the neighbors were either gone or staying home.

Drifting on the damp air came the scent of wood smoke and Tommy breathed deeply. He'd given up smoking more than a year ago. It had taken him six months to get from five cigarettes a day to none. He'd think it was completely out of his system, and then he'd catch a whiff of smoke—even the sour stench of burning leaves—and want a cigarette so badly he could taste it. Kiki's slow intake of breath, a signal that she was about to speak again, doubled the desire.

"How long do we wait?"

"The guy might have had car trouble. He might have gotten a late start, or the weather might have slowed him down."

"Or your informant might have given you bad information. He might have just liked the idea of us sitting out here in the rain waiting for something that was never going to happen in the first place."

"Maybe."

She repeated her question. "So how long do we wait?"

"As long as it takes." She was probably right. This bust was a bust. But just to keep her from thinking she'd nagged him into giving up, he waited another half hour before finally starting the engine. The Dodge Charger turned with a powerful rumble, and he pulled out of the trees and drove away from Terrell's house.

Kiki gave an exaggerated sigh of relief, then looked slyly at him. "I saw you at Ellie's last night with Sophy."

"Yeah." Tommy resisted the urge to fidget. His dating Sophy

wasn't a secret. He'd been seeing her for a month, though he'd never taken her to the deli. Though he'd been a regular since the doors opened, taking his current girlfriend to his ex-girlfriend's restaurant seemed a really lousy idea. Last night the choice hadn't been his. Anamaria had been craving prime rib, and Ellie's was the best in town.

He missed the food there. Almost as much as he missed Ellie.

"Sophy and I are friends. If you break her heart, I'll have to shoot you."

After turning onto Carolina Avenue, he gave Kiki a sharp look, then deliberately changed the subject. "I'm taking you back to the station. Then I'm going looking for my informant."

"I'll go with you."

"No, thanks."

"Come on, Maricci—"

"He's called a confidential informant for a reason. Besides, you wouldn't like the places he hangs out."

"Tommy—"

He pulled to a stop in front of the Copper Lake Police Department and waited pointedly for her to get out of the car. When she didn't move, he said, "Go inside, Kiki. Do your nails or fix your hair or something. I'll swing back after I'm done."

With a scowl, she climbed out, muttering something about macho jerks and pissants. Grinning, he pulled out of the parking lot and headed back downtown. He did intend to go looking for his informant, but not until he'd gotten something to eat, along with a strong cup of coffee.

He circled halfway around the square before finding a parking space near A Cuppa Joe. As he got out of the Charger, a figure crossing the street caught his attention. She wore a long coat that was too big, the hood pulled up over gray hair and a lined face, and trudged through the crosswalk with a plastic shopping bag clutched in each hand.

It was the woman Ellie had been talking to on the porch last night, the out-of-towner who wanted something from her. Ellie hadn't been happy to see her or to talk about her with him in the square…though these days she wasn't happy talking about anything with him.

On impulse, he met the woman as she stepped onto the curb. "Can I help you with your bags?"

She drew up short and fixed a suspicious stare on him. "Do I look like I need help?"

"No, ma'am. I just thought—"

"Who are you?"

"Tommy Maricci." He gestured to the gold shield clipped onto his belt, and her gaze dropped, then returned to his face. "I haven't done nothin' wrong."

"I didn't say you had. I just thought you might like some help. Maybe a ride to get out of this rain." A blast of wind kicked up behind her, bringing with it the smell of stale smoke and liquor.

Shifting the bags to one hand, she raised the other to tug her hood back enough to see him better. "You always offer innocent strangers rides?"

"More often than you'd think."

"Huh. All right. I'll take your ride." She handed both bags to him, then shoved her hands into her coat pockets. "It *is* a bit chilly for this time of year. And I'm not going far. Just to the Jasmine."

Her blue eyes narrowed, clearly expecting some response from him, but he was good at hiding surprise. The Jasmine was a restored three-storied brick-and-plaster post–Civil War beauty on two prime acres east of downtown. Now a bed-and-breakfast, it was by far the most expensive place to stay in Copper Lake. Not what he would have expected for this woman.

Though his job had taught him to expect the unexpected.

"My car's over there." He gestured toward the Charger, and they'd walked a few yards when she inhaled deeply.

"Nothing smells as good on a chilly day as a cup of strong coffee."

Especially with a little something extra in it to help warm a body, he thought, catching another whiff of alcohol. "I was just heading for a cup. Do you have time?"

Her laughter was throaty and grating. "I have nothin' but time. Are you treating?"

"Sure."

"Well, then, why don't you put them bags up and I'll wait inside out of the cold?" Without pausing for his agreement, she pivoted and walked into A Cuppa Joe.

Tommy unlocked the car door and set the bags in the back. As the plastic sides sagged, he saw two cartons of cigarettes, a six-pack of beer, chips and three large bags of candy. Tucked between the beer and the *Enquirer* was a slim brown bag, the kind used at the local liquor stores. Booze, chocolate and a gossip rag…the basic requirements of life.

After closing and locking the door, he strode down the sidewalk and into the coffee shop. The woman was standing at the counter, head tilted back, studying the menu on the wall. She'd pushed the hood off her head, leaving her hair sticking out like tufts of straw, and, like the night before, she gave off an air of watchfulness. "Does that offer go for plain coffee or the grande-mocha-latte-chino good stuff?"

"Whatever you want."

A twenty-something girl with bottled black hair and deep purple lips waited idly for their order, tapping an orange fingernail on the counter. A person could be forgiven for thinking she was already in the Halloween spirit, but she looked like that every day of the year. After the woman ordered a caramel-hazelnut something-or-other, Tommy asked for his usual— high-octane Brazilian blend with a slice of cream-cheese-filled pumpkin bread.

"Make that two slices," the woman said with a sly smile. "I'll find a table."

Midafternoon, with only a couple of other customers, that was no hardship. She chose one near the front window but away from the draft of the door. By the time Tommy set down the tray with their food, she'd removed her coat and sat, legs crossed, hands clasped on the tabletop. Her fingers were short, stubby and nicotine stained, her nails blunt and unpolished. The skin on her hands, like on her face, was weathered and worn. Not by work, he suspected. She didn't strike him as a woman who indulged in hard work.

And she didn't strike him as a woman who would have even the vaguest connection to Ellie. Ellie was so elegant and polished and...just *different*.

"I didn't get your name," he said as he set a tall foamy cup and a saucer with bread in front of her.

"I didn't offer it." She swiped a finger in the whipped cream that topped her drink, licked it clean, then shrugged. "Martha Dempsey."

"Are you here on vacation? Visiting friends? Just passing through?"

Picking up her fork, she wagged it in his direction. "That's the bad thing about cops. They're always asking questions."

"We're just curious people." And he wasn't asking even a fraction of the questions running through his mind. *Who are you? Why are you here? How do you know Ellie? What do you want from her?*

"I seen you last night. At the restaurant down the street. With that pregnant black girl. Is she *your* girl?" There was an undertone of something—disapproval, bigotry—that made her voice coarse, ugly.

"I like to think she could have been if my buddy hadn't met her first." He'd liked Anamaria from the first time they'd met, but Robbie, she insisted, had been her destiny. God knows, she'd certainly turned him around. The shallow Calloway brother, the irresponsible one, had taken to marriage and impending fatherhood as well as or better than any of his more responsible brothers.

"She's not your kind," Martha said dismissively.

Before he could ask just how she meant that, she shifted her gaze outside to a temporary sign in the square, announcing the date and time of the annual Halloween celebration. "This isn't a bad little town. I'm thinking I could live out my last days here."

And what would Ellie think of that? "I've lived all my days here, except for four years in college. I like it." He stirred sugar into his coffee, then took a careful sip before asking, "Where do you live now?"

"Atlanta. Big place. You can stay twenty years in the same house and still not know your neighbor's name." She gave him another of those sly looks. "I bet you know pretty much everything about everyone in town. Or, at least, you think you do."

"I'm not sure you can ever know *everything* about a person." He was probably the only one in town who didn't have much in the way of secrets. The only major events in his life—his mother's alcoholism, her leaving when he was five and abandoning him, his falling in love with Ellie and her not loving him back—were common knowledge. He had nothing to hide.

"What do you know about Ellie Chase?"

He stilled in the act of reaching for another bite of pumpkin bread. Laying his fork carefully on the plate, he folded his hands around his coffee cup instead. "She's got the best restaurant in town. Everyone likes her. She's good to work for. She's active in the community." He paused. "I know you know her."

Ellie hadn't actually said that. Martha Dempsey was just someone who wanted something, she'd said. Someone from the past she never talked about, he'd inferred.

Martha's smile was crooked. "A long time ago," she said. "I hadn't seen her since she was a teenager."

"Is she the reason you came here?"

She studied him a moment, then took a drink of coffee, slurping to get whipped cream, as well. With a drop clinging to her upper lip, she said, "What you call curiosity, Mr. Police Detective, some people consider plain old nosiness."

"Is she?"

After another drink, she shook her head. "Her being here is just a happy coincidence."

"I don't believe in coincidence." And Ellie certainly hadn't seemed happy.

That earned a sharp laugh from her. "I don't believe in little green men from Mars, neither, but that don't mean they aren't out there. Now...tell me about this Halloween festival."

A shrill whistle startled Ellie, who'd been staring off into the distance. She shifted her gaze to the door of her office where Sherry, one of the waitresses, stood, a takeout bag in hand.

"I called your name three times. You imagining yourself on some Caribbean beach with a hot cabana boy?"

If only her mind had wandered someplace so pleasant... But no, she'd been distant in years, not so much in mileage. "You bet," she lied, forcing a smile. "The sun was warm, the sand was endless and the rum never stopped flowing."

"Well, come back to reality, where the sky is gray, the temperature is cold and the rain hasn't stopped falling." Sherry held up the bag. "Joe's order is ready."

Ellie looked blankly at the bag before remembering: Joe Saldana had called in an order to go, and she'd offered to deliver it to him. He'd promised her a tall chai tea, his own special blend, as a fee.

"I can take it for you."

"You're married, Sherry," Ellie reminded her as she rose from the chair, then took her jacket from the coat tree in the corner.

"But there's no harm in looking."

The waitress handed over the bag, and the fragrant aromas of the day's special—roasted chicken, dressing, mashed potatoes and gravy, along with a piece of apple pie—drifted into the air. It was enough to remind Ellie that she had skipped lunch, and breakfast, as well. She hadn't been able to stomach the idea of food.

Not with the sour stenches of fear, bourbon and nicotine that had gripped her for the past fifteen hours or so.

"I'll tell Joe you send your regards," she said as she squeezed past Sherry and started down the hall.

"Oh, honey," Sherry murmured behind her. "I want to give him a whole lot more than that."

Ellie's faint smile faded before she reached the door. They'd had a busy lunch, and one of the staff had called in sick, so she'd had to pitch in and wait tables. Busy was good; it kept her from thinking about anything more than the task at hand.

But busy couldn't last forever, and once the lunch rush was over, she'd retreated to her office and brooded. She'd faced a lot of problems in her life, but there had always been solutions. This one had solutions, too—just none that she could face at the moment.

The rain came in steady, small *plops* against her lemon-yellow slicker until she reached the protection of the awnings that fronted the other businesses on the block. There she pushed the hood back and drew in a deep breath of fresh, clean air. Speaking to the few people she passed on the sidewalk, Ellie realized with some measure of surprise that she would miss Copper Lake if she had to leave. She'd tried not to get overly attached to the town or the people in it. *Home* was a concept, not a place, and people let you down. From the day she'd come there, she'd wanted to be able to leave without regret.

Tried. Wanted. Truth was, she *was* attached. She could own another dozen restaurants, and none of them would mean the same as the deli. She could make a hundred new friends, but they would never replace Anamaria and Jamie, the Calloways, Carmen and everyone else. She could have a thousand more affairs, but not one of them—

Grimly she stopped herself midthought as the fragrance of fresh-roasted coffee drifted into her senses. A Cuppa Joe occupied the corner lot, a full block from her own place. Ironically, Joe Saldana hadn't named the gourmet shop. It was just coincidence that Joe now owned A Cuppa Joe.

I don't believe in coincidence.

Scowling at the words she'd heard more than once from Tommy, she pushed open the plate-glass door and went inside. Louis Armstrong played softly on the stereo—Joe didn't listen to anything recorded after 1960—and coffee scents perfumed the air.

She was halfway across the shop, already anticipating the first sip of chai tea, when she realized that something was amiss. Slowing her steps, Ellie glanced over her shoulder, then came to an abrupt stop and turned.

Martha was sitting at the front table farthest from the door. With Tommy.

A chill shivered through her as she stared at them and they stared back. There was malice in Martha's expression, speculation and something more in Tommy's. A little longing. Maybe regret. Definitely curiosity.

How had they wound up in the coffee shop together? Had it been Tommy's doing, his way of finding out answers she hadn't given him the night before? Or had Martha sought him out? Did she somehow know they'd been involved?

Ellie couldn't speak, couldn't move or look away, until Joe's voice broke the shock that held her.

"Hey, Ellie. How much do I owe you?"

Bit by bit, she forced her attention from Tommy and Martha to Joe, who was sliding his wallet from his hip pocket as he came out from behind the counter. She tried to remember how much the lunch special was, but couldn't. Gratefully, though, she recognized the ticket nestled atop the foam container in the plastic bag and pulled it out, handing it over.

"Nina's getting your tea," Joe said, offering her a ten-dollar bill in exchange for the bag. "Why don't you come on back with me?"

Ellie still felt Tommy's and Martha's gazes, though, prickling down her spine and into her somersaulting stomach as Joe took her arm, guiding her behind the counter. She numbly went along. As soon as they reached the rear space that served as both store-room and office, he closed the door and the prickling went away.

He released her, went to the battered desk and unpacked his lunch. "So you and Maricci still aren't friendly."

She shook her head.

"I doubt you have to worry much about the woman with him. She's not his type."

He was wrong. Martha was the biggest worry in her life.

"Okay, bad joke. What's wrong? This is hardly the first time you've seen him since…" With typical male tact, he shrugged instead of finishing. *Since he walked away from you. Since he gave up on you.*

"It's not that," she said, and it was only half a lie. She could handle seeing Tommy. She could even handle seeing him with Sophy. But with Martha, who hadn't been satisfied with ruining her life fifteen years ago? Who'd come to Copper Lake for the sole purpose of ruining what was left?

"Then what is it?" Joe asked as he cut a generous bite of chicken.

"Complicated," she said with a helpless shrug.

"Sex always is."

Leave it to a man to boil down her and Tommy's relationship to its most basic component. If it were only sex, they would have no problem, because the sex was always good.

"And how's your sex life?" she asked to change the subject.

"I'm thinking about it."

She snorted. In the year since he'd come to town, he'd caught the eye of every available woman—and a few who weren't. Six foot four, tanned, muscular, with unruly blond hair and blue eyes, he could have women lined up around the block. *Had* had women lined up the day he'd reopened A Cuppa Joe after remodeling. But to the best of her knowledge, he'd never gone out with any of them. He was friendly, considerate and disinterested.

"How long can a man go without?" she asked.

His forehead wrinkled for a moment, then smoothed. "Eighteen months, two weeks and three days. And counting."

She gazed at him a long time, while he sampled the mashed potatoes, dipped a forkful of dressing into the gravy, then cut another piece of chicken. Finally she shook her head and started toward the rear wall. "Can I use your back door?"

"You gonna slink back down the alley to the diner? Coward." But he gestured toward the door with careless approval.

She let herself out the door with a wave, then stood underneath the roof overhang while pulling the slicker hood into place. Hands shoved into her pockets, she turned left toward the deli, but after a dozen feet, turned around and headed along the sidewalk in the other direction instead. Shivering more than the weather called for, she turned at the next block and headed aimlessly out of the business district and into a neighborhood of lovely old homes.

Five years ago Ellie had chosen Copper Lake as her new home based on only one thing: the two-hundred-year-old general store turned restaurant turned hot investment property. Randolph Aiken, her mentor, for lack of a better word, had contacted her in Charleston, where she'd been working for a friend of his in a lush, plush, black-tie restaurant and told her about the space. It would be a great investment, he'd said, for that money she'd been saving.

Payoff money.

When she'd driven through Copper Lake that first time, her initial thought had been that it was too pretty, too small-town perfect. She didn't belong in such a place.

But she hadn't fit in in Charleston, either, or Atlanta. She didn't belong anywhere, so she might as well not belong in Copper Lake, where she could have her own modest restaurant.

Then something strange had happened along the way. The town and its people had made a place for her. They'd welcomed her, befriended her and treated her like any normal person.

Tommy's welcome had been the sweetest.

A short, sharp tap of a car horn sounded as she was about to cross a driveway. She drew up short, realizing she'd reached the Jasmine, one of Copper Lake's historic gems, as an elegant gray Mercedes glided to a stop in front of her. The driver rolled down the window, and both he and the passenger, the inn's owners, smiled up at her. "Look at this, Jared. It's the middle of the afternoon, and Ellie Chase is out taking a stroll," Jeffrey Goldman said.

"Let me mark this date on the calendar. I do believe it's a first," Jared Franklin replied.

Ellie couldn't help but smile at both men. Like her, like Joe Saldana, they'd come to Copper Lake to make a new start. Unlike her and Joe, everyone knew the basic facts of their lives. They were open and unashamed; they had nothing to hide.

"I'm not at the deli *all* the time," she protested.

"No, of course not," Jeffrey agreed. "You have to sleep sometime."

"You're not still sleeping on that couch in your office, are you?" Jared asked.

"One time. And it was just a nap. I'd worked late the night before for… What was it? Oh, yeah, *your* birthday party." Ironic that a birthday party for a retired lawyer had turned into the largest and most boisterous private event the restaurant had ever hosted. The sheer number of people who'd made the drive from Atlanta had been astounding—lawyers, judges, criminals. She'd spent half the night in the kitchen, afraid she would run into someone who'd known her from before.

That was no way to live, but if she gave in to Martha's black-mail demands, she would live the rest of her life just like that.

"Why don't you let us give you a ride to wherever you're going?" Jeffrey asked.

She was about to say no, thanks, when another car approached. It was black and looked so unlike a police car, she had once teased, that of course it was. The turn signal was on, the driver—Tommy, of course—preparing to turn into the Jasmine's other entrance, the one that circled around to the small guest parking area. In the passenger seat, a glimpse of sallow skin and tufty gray hair proved that Martha was still with him.

It was hard to walk off your problems when they kept showing up.

Turning her gaze back to the men, Ellie smiled. "If you're not worried that I'll ruin your upholstery, I would like a ride back to the deli."

"Upholstery can be cleaned," Jeffrey said with a negligible wave.

The electric locks clicked, and she opened the rear door before either man could get out to do so for her. As she slid onto the buttery leather seat, the Charger disappeared behind a hedge of neatly groomed azaleas.

"Do you have a guest named Martha?" she asked, striving for a conversational tone as the Mercedes began moving again.

Jared's nose twitched subtly. "Yes, we do."

"She came to the restaurant last night. Wow. I couldn't afford to stay at your place unless you hired me as the live-in help. I guess appearances really can be deceiving."

Jeffrey ignored Jared's snort. "She has money. We have rooms. And you know, we'd always cut you a deal, Ellie. You're our favorite restaurant owner in town."

"She has money, all right," Jared said. "She paid for a week from a thick stack of hundred-dollar bills. Said she'd never stayed in a place quite so fancy." He put a twang on the last few words that should have made Ellie smile, but didn't.

Where had Martha gotten a stack of hundred-dollar bills? Had Oliver had life insurance enough for her to bury him, pay her usual bills and allow her to splurge on a two-hundred-dollar-a-night bed-and-breakfast? Maybe she hadn't wasted any money on a burial. After all, he was no use to her dead.

Just as her daughter had been no use to her.

It didn't make sense. If Martha needed money—and she must; how else would she survive with her aversion to work?—why wasn't she staying at the Riverview Motel? One night at the Jasmine would cover nearly a week at the Riverview.

Thinking about it made her head hurt. Thinking about Martha with Tommy made it hurt worse.

Staring out the window, she listened to Jeffrey and Jared's idle chatter until they reached the restaurant. She thanked them for the ride and climbed out into heavier rain.

"Next time you need a break from work, come on over," Jared invited. "I'll fix you my special Long Island iced tea, and we'll dish on *all* the guests. I could tell you things…"

Politely she said she would, then hurried along the sidewalk and up the steps to the porch. As she shrugged out of her slicker, she remembered that she'd forgotten to pick up her chai tea at A Cuppa Joe.

Too bad. She could have used it.

* * *

Tommy didn't feel guilty for taking care of personal matters on department time. He put in way more than his forty hours a week, routinely getting called out too early in the morning and too late at night, to say nothing of spending more than a fair amount of his evenings writing and reading reports, studying notes and trying to figure out why people did the things they did.

The rain had stopped after he'd dropped Martha Dempsey off at the Jasmine, and now the sun was making a so-so stab at breaking through the clouds in the western sky. Finding no space on the square, he parked in Robbie's law office lot and jogged across the street, careful not to spill the still-warm chai tea in the cup he carried.

Ellie's Deli sat fifteen feet back from the sidewalk, the path to the steps flanked on both sides with beds of yellow and purple pansies. Those had been his mother's favorite flowers, back in the days when she'd found the energy to plant anything at all, and his father had continued to plant them for years. The autumn he'd stopped, Tommy thought, was when he'd finally accepted that Lilah wasn't coming back.

By then, she'd been gone for eleven years.

Like father, like son. Mooning endlessly over women who didn't want them.

The main dining room was empty except for a half dozen girls gathered in one corner wearing the uniform of Copper Lake High School cheerleaders, and a waitress, poring over a textbook while waiting for something to do.

"Is Ellie here?"

The waitress, a high school student herself, nodded before a burst of laughter drew her gaze, a bit longing, to the girls. It wasn't fun, Tommy would bet, having to wait on the cool kids. Thanks to his friendship with Robbie, he'd been one of the cool kids in school, for all the difference it made. Some of them had gone on to achieve a lot; some of them were regular visitors at the Copper Lake Correctional Facility.

"She's in her office," the girl said. "I'll get her—"

"That's okay. I know the way." He passed through the main dining room, past the bathrooms and the bar, dimly lit for now, until the evening bartender came on at five, then stopped at the next door. For more than four years, he'd been in the habit of walking right in, without a knock or warning. But such familiarity didn't seem appropriate at the moment.

Then his jaw tightened. How had his life come to this, that familiarity with the one woman he knew better than himself wasn't appropriate?

He rapped at the door, sharper than he'd intended to, and a quiet invitation followed. "Come in."

He could do the polite thing: give the tea to the girl up front and let her deliver it. Or the smart thing: toss the cup in the nearest trash can and beat it out the back door. But he didn't stand a chance trying to find out what he wanted to know by being polite, and he couldn't spend even a moment with her if he slipped out the back door the way she had earlier. So he twisted the knob, let himself in and closed the door behind him.

Ellie was a hands-on manager, chatting with the guests, refilling drinks, clearing tables, delivering food and even, on a regular basis, rolling up her sleeves in the kitchen. She knew every job as well as her employees and was energetic enough that she could run the place sans two or three of them without showing the strain.

This afternoon, as she sat alone in her office, doing nothing, the strain showed.

He set the chai tea on the middle of the desk pad, nudged the visitor chair with one boot toe, then took a few steps back to lean instead against a narrow oak table that butted up to the wall. "Nina said you forgot that."

She didn't touch the cup. "She could have delivered it herself or just thrown it away."

"She was too busy." Joe's was a popular place after school, with its wireless Internet connections and doctored drinks that tasted more like dessert than coffee. Besides, Tommy hadn't given her much of a chance. *She left without her tea,* Nina had complained, and he'd been quick to respond. *I'll take it to her.*

Martha Dempsey had given him a look, part slyness, part meanness and part curiosity. He'd ignored her. Though ignoring Martha Dempsey too often, he figured, was the express route to trouble.

Ellie looked at it a moment as if she might do what he hadn't: throw it away. She even picked it up and started to turn to the side, but the wisps of steam drifting up from the small hole in the lid were rich with cinnamon and cloves. Instead of completing the move toward the wastebasket behind her desk, she lifted the cover, wrapped both hands around the still-warm cup and breathed deeply. After taking a tentative sip, then a long, savoring drink, she grudgingly said, "Thank you."

He watched her, taking far too much pleasure in her pleasure, growing warm inside his jacket, remembering not long ago when he would have made some suggestive comment, when she would have responded with suggestiveness of her own. Back when they were together. When he'd thought they had a chance.

He waited until she lowered the cup again to remark, "You saw that I had coffee with Martha Dempsey."

Darkness eased into Ellie's features—nothing so obvious as a scowl, just a subtle displeasure, dislike, distrust. If he didn't know her so well, he probably would have missed it. "Your idea or hers?"

"Mine. I'm a cop, Ellie. I get answers one way or another."

"And what answers are you looking for about her?"

"She's new in town. She looks like she doesn't have a dime,

but she's staying at the Jasmine. And just the sight of her upsets you." He shrugged. "All that makes me curious."

"You could mind your own business."

Though she was totally serious, he laughed. "I haven't minded my own business since I was five years old. That's why I became a cop in the first place." He'd always wanted answers, and if he didn't get them the usual way, he found them another.

"Martha said she hasn't seen you since you were a teenager. That her coming to Copper Lake and finding you here is a happy coincidence."

When neither comment drew a response from her, Tommy fired off a third one, embellished for effect. "She said she's looking forward to living out her life here, close to you."

Something flashed in Ellie's eyes, and a muscle convulsed in her jaw with the effort to keep her mouth shut, but she succeeded. After a moment, with a faintly strangled quality to her voice, she replied, "It's a free country. She can move wherever she wants."

"Why wouldn't you want her here?"

"Why would I? I hardly know the woman, and I have no desire to get to know her better."

"Where do you know her from?"

A heavy silence developed as Ellie studied him. Her chin was lifted, the soft swing of her pale hair brushing the delicate skin there. Her heart rate had settled to its usual throb, visible at the base of her throat, and her features looked as if they had been carved from ice.

Finally she rose from the desk, circling to the front, mimicking his pose. Her hips rested against the worn oak, her ankles crossed, her fingers still cradling the tea. "She's from my father's past," she said flatly. "Not mine."

Maybe two yards of dull pine separated their feet. As relaxed as she looked, it should be an easy thing to push away from the table and reach her before she could think about retreating. But her ease was deceptive. If he so much as breathed deeply, she would be an instant from fleeing.

In five years she hadn't talked a lot about her parents. Her upbringing had been boringly conventional. Mother, father and only child, blue house not far from the beach, across the Cooper River from Charleston. Mother had died in a car wreck eight or ten years ago, father soon after of a heart attack. Normal life. No unusual traumas, no major dramas.

And he'd had no reason to doubt her. For every person who found comfort in talking about times that were past and people who were gone, there was one who found it tough. Some memories were better kept to oneself.

She's from my father's past.

Some hurts, like a father's betrayal of a mother, were better buried.

Silence settled, as if one confidence was all she had in her. He wished he could close that six-foot distance, earn another secret or even just a moment being silent together. Six months ago he could have held her, and she would have let him. Let him, but not opened to him. There had always been distance between them, that had pushed them apart time after time, that had caused him to finally give her an ultimatum: commit or end it. All or nothing.

Saying "I want everything" was a hell of a lot easier than living with nothing.

"Well…" They both spoke at once, both broke off at once. Ellie moved away from the desk. "I've got things to do…."

"Yeah. Me, too." Still, it took an effort for him to move. He wished she would walk past him and into the hall. Not too close. Just enough that her clothing would brush his, that her perfume would tickle his nose.

She didn't, though, instead returning to her desk, focusing her attention on the paperwork there. Grimly, he walked out.

Chapter 3

When Ellie walked onto the porch Friday afternoon, the sun was shining, making it warm enough for short sleeves. After the previous day's rain, everything downtown had a fresh, clean look to it: the color of the flowers brighter, the contrast against the grass sharper, the smells of sawn wood richer and earthier. The news reports called for good weather through the weekend, with an appropriate fall crackle in the air on Saturday for the Copper Lake Halloween Festival.

The sound of rhythmic hammering came from the square where a half-dozen teams of volunteers were building the booths for the festival. Most of the local restaurants sponsored a booth; Ellie's was a prime corner section, directly across the street from the deli. There would also be the usual carnival-type food—funnel cakes, Sno-Cones, deep-fried everything—and simple old-fashioned games like bobbing for apples and musical chairs. There would be costume parades across the front veranda of River's Edge, the grand Greek Revival plantation home on the southeast side of the square, and a band would set up in the gazebo.

A lot of good fun for kids and their families and people who had dates, she thought sourly.

A sleek vintage Corvette pulled to the curb at the end of the walk, top down in deference to the weather. Her hair tied back with a red print scarf, Anamaria looked exotic and sexy as usual. She was a beautiful woman, and deeply in love with her husband. Those Calloway boys—and their wives—had all the luck.

Ellie slid into the passenger seat. "I thought you didn't like to drive the 'Vette."

"Oh, I like to," Anamaria replied breezily. "I just don't like Robbie to know."

Robbie was inordinately proud of the vehicle he'd bought as little more than a rusted heap and rebuilt from the ground up. Since his marriage to Anamaria, it had been a sore point that she preferred to drive her nothing-special Honda over his restored baby.

"Besides," Anamaria said, resting one hand lightly on the swelling of her stomach, "I figure if I want to drive it, I'd better do it before Gloriane gets too big."

Ellie's gaze dropped to Anamaria's belly; then she pointedly looked away. She never thought about having children. Never. It was safer that way. Well, except when she saw an expectant mother or a sweet, innocent infant. Or when she watched Russ and Jamie fussing over two-month-old Sara Elizabeth. Or noticed how solicitous Robbie was of Anamaria. Or let her defenses down and remembered back to when she was a child herself and for such a very short time, things had seemed…hopeful.

For a moment she closed her eyes, grinding her teeth, shoring up that little bit of weakness around her heart. When Anamaria's hand settled on her arm, it startled her eyes open again.

"Are you all right?"

It was such an easy question to lie to. She'd been doing it for years—smiling, tossing off an airy *I'm fine*. Truthfully, for a good portion of the past five years, she *had* been fine. She'd had more in her life—a career, a home, a good man and dear friends—than she'd ever dreamed of.

Now, thanks to Martha, it was hard to imagine that anything would ever be *fine* again.

Still, she managed an uneven smile. "I'm fine. How is Mama Odette?"

Anamaria clearly recognized the question for the evasive tactic it was, but let it slide. "She's great. The doctors say she's got the heart of a woman half her age." After a pause, she went on with a sly smile. "And Mama Odette says she's not giving it back."

Ellie laughed in the moment before her thoughts took a melancholy turn. Anamaria had never known her father, and her mother had died when she was a little girl. But she'd had an amazing family welcoming her with open arms—her grandmother, Odette; her aunts and their daughters; Odette's sisters and their daughters. Dozens of strong, smart and loving Duquesne women gathering her in.

And Ellie had had her mother and her father, neither of whom had wanted kids in the first place. Her paternal grandmother had been a cigar-smoking, whiskey-drinking old woman who'd scared the wits out of Ellie every chance she got, and her maternal grandparents had never been a part of her life. She'd had aunts and uncles but could hardly remember them, had cousins but had never known them.

It wasn't fair—all those people who'd loved Anamaria, and not even one who'd wanted Ellie.

Life ain't fair, Martha had often said as she'd unscrewed the cap from yet another bottle of booze.

The *click* of the turn signal penetrated Ellie's thoughts, and she looked up to see that they'd reached the mall. It was small, but it offered a lot, including their reason for coming there. In a small first-level storefront was the Seasonal Store. If you celebrated a holiday, any holiday, the Seasonal Store was the place to shop. Right now the front half was filled with all things Halloween, while in the rear, Christmas was encroaching on the space allocated to Thanksgiving.

"You shouldn't have put off buying your costume for so long," Anamaria admonished as they wound through the racks. "There's not a lot left for adults."

"Are you dressing up?" It had taken Ellie's staff three years to nag her into joining them among the ranks of the costumed. She'd had fun. She'd felt free. She had looked forward to repeating it this year…until things had changed.

"Of course I am," Anamaria replied, then added drama to her voice. "I'm going as the great Queen Moon, who knows all, hears all and sees all, but doesn't tell all for less than a gold doubloon." She took a costume from the rack, studied it a moment, then returned it to pick up a different garment. "There really was a Moon in our family—she was Mama Odette's great-grandmother—and her faithful believers really did call her Queen. Who knows? Maybe I'll channel her Saturday night."

Psychic gifts ran strong in the Duquesne family. It had made Ellie wary when she'd first met Anamaria. Could Anamaria see things that no one else could? she'd wondered. Would she give away secrets Ellie had so stubbornly kept?

The answers, the last six months had determined: seeing secrets? Probably. Sharing them? Definitely not.

"How about this?"

Ellie turned away from a moldy-looking corpse outfit to find Anamaria holding a full black skirt. She lifted one flirty strip of nearly transparent fabric, then let it flutter down again. "Just a skirt?"

"I have a white peasant top you can borrow and a burgundy velvet shawl with fringe. And some black knee boots, a scarf to tie over your hair, maybe a long wig and voilà."

"Voilà what?" Ellie asked drily. "Serving wench? Pirate lady?"

"Depending on how low we can get the neck of the blouse, maybe pirate's lady friend," Anamaria teased.

"I think she was closer the first time with wench," a voice said from behind Ellie. "After all, isn't that just an old-fashioned way of saying whore?"

Ellie restrained the impulse to whirl around. She didn't need to look to know it was Martha who had spoken, didn't need to give her the satisfaction of knowing she'd caught Ellie off-guard.

Anamaria gave Martha a long, level look, then took hold of Ellie's arm. "Let's find a wig."

Ellie's feet automatically followed Anamaria's lead, but Martha wasn't about to be ignored.

"You're that psychic girl that's married to the youngest Calloway boy, aren't you? Man, you must have put some mighty good voodoo on him, getting him to marry you, what with him being rich and white and you being neither." Martha fluffed her hair and smiled broadly. "What does your psychic gift say about me?"

"Just ignore her," Ellie said, but Anamaria wasn't listening.

She walked in a slow circle around Martha. "Your whole life, you've cared for no one but yourself. You've disappointed and hurt all those who should have mattered to you. But there's still time to change. You can't undo the past, but you can change the future."

Martha's eyes widened for an instant; then her laughter sounded, loud and coarse. "I surely do intend to change my future. Wow, you really must be psychic or something. Don't you think, Ellie?"

Ellie's face was hot, her stomach knotted. She wanted to

stick her fingers in her ears so she would never have to hear that voice or that laughter again, wanted to scrub her eyes with her knuckles to chase away the sight of that smug, vicious face. But she would never be free of Martha now that the woman had tracked her down, so running was next on her list of desires. She'd even taken a step back when Martha's gaze shifted past her, and the woman gave a friendly wave.

"There's Reverend Fitzgerald's wife, Kayla. Such a nice girl. We met at the church this morning—I dropped in for a little meditation time—and she invited me to go shopping with her. She needs a birthday gift for her mother-in-law, who's about my age. Thanks for the advice, Anamaria. And, Ellie—" her blue gaze sharpened "—I'll be seeing you around."

Ellie wondered if Anamaria heard the threat in those last words as clearly as she did. Martha was doing a very good job of insinuating herself into the lives of Ellie's friends. They were nice people; they'd never suspect her of having an ulterior motive. And once she'd weaseled her way in, how much easier would it be for her to convince them of the truth of her tales about Ellie? She would paint herself the victim, the loving mother who had tried so desperately to help her out-of-control daughter, and people would have no choice but to believe her.

And she had proof.

Once Martha exited into the mall, the air inside the shop became easier to breathe. Ellie took a cleansing breath, chasing away the last of the cigarette and booze odor, and found Anamaria studying her somberly, her dark eyes troubled.

"Who is she, Ellie?"

Numbly she shook her head, then dug some nonchalance from deep inside. "Just some wacko who seems to have fixated on me. No big deal."

"As I recall, the last wacko in town who fixated on someone tried to kill both my brother- and sister-in-law. The Calloway family in general and Russ and Jamie in particular considered it a very big deal."

"This woman's not violent." Not beyond a slap now and then. The occasional physical violence had been easier to endure than Martha's relentlessly cold treatment. Bruises healed. Emotional scars didn't.

"That's what they thought about Lys Paxton until she started trying to kill people."

Ellie moved past displays of candy, spiders and webs, camouflage face paint and long fake fingernails in deep purple, black and bloodred, and Anamaria followed. "Martha Dempsey is many things," she said, shooting for a breezy tone, "but she's not a killer."

"What is she to you?"

"A blast from the past. How's this?" Stopping in front of a selection of cheap wigs, Ellie picked up one from the top row and clamped it onto her head. The mirror next to the display showed a fringe of brow-brushing bangs and a straight fall of silken strands that ended past her shoulders. The jet-black hue gave her skin a sickly blue tinge.

"Unless you're going as a wench of the undead, that is so not your color," Anamaria teased. "Try this."

She handed over another long wig, this one dark copper and curly. The color wasn't as surprising a contrast as the black wig, but it was different enough to be fun. She pulled it off again and combed her fingers through her own blond hair. "Let me pay for this and the skirt, then let's get out of here." She didn't want to run into Martha again and certainly didn't want to be reminded how easily the woman was finding welcome in Ellie's own town.

She'd checked out and they were walking back through the mall to the entrance when a laugh echoed across the space. She tried to ignore it, but her gaze traveled that direction anyway, to the few occupied tables at the sidewalk café that fronted the fountain. Kayla Fitzgerald sat at one, her smile serene, and Martha sat to her left. At the next table, chairs turned for easier conversation, were Sara Calloway and Jack Greyson, the man she old-fashionedly referred to as her beau.

A chill swept over Ellie. Kayla was the pastor's wife; she had to be nice to strangers. But Sara was Anamaria's mother-in-law. More important, she was the closest thing to a mother Tommy had ever had.

She's taunting you, a voice in Ellie's head whispered. *She's saying, "Look how easily I can get to them, and there's only one way you can stop me."*

Only one way to Martha's way of thinking: give her money and trust her to go away…until the money ran out and she needed more. Ellie could give her everything and still never buy her silence.

If there was just some way to get rid of her for good…

Get rid of her. The words echoed across the years, hurtful, yet another betrayal to a girl who'd already experienced too many. They slowed her steps until she was hardly moving.

Ellie didn't have a clue how to manipulate and control people, but she knew someone who did. Part of Randolph Aiken's duties as lawyer to his respectable and influential Old South family had involved persuading people who might prove cause for embarrassment to disappear, to keep their distance from and their silence about the family.

People like Ellie.

She didn't know if Randolph had taken a liking to all the people he threatened on behalf of the Aikens, but his attitude toward her had always been somewhat paternal. He'd given her advice, stayed in touch with her long after she'd expected him to vanish, had helped her move to Charleston and put her life back together. It was his contacts that had gotten her her first job, his assistance that had led to her owning her own restaurant.

He would surely have some suggestion for what to do about Martha.

"Ellie? Are you coming?"

The sound of Anamaria's voice made her blink. While she'd come to a complete stop, Anamaria had reached the double glass doors ahead and was holding one open, watching her curiously.

Ellie hastily moved forward, sweeping through the door, then held the outer door in turn. "I'm all right," she said before Anamaria could ask. "I really am."

And for the first time since she'd seen Martha standing on the deli's porch, she somewhat believed it.

Every year Tommy took off work on the Friday before the Halloween festival, trading his badge and pistol for a hammer and nails, and this year was no exception. Sara Calloway chaired the committee in charge of the festival, and she knew she could always count on her boys—a designation that included him—to work.

He was helping Robbie and Russ knock together the last of the booths when he heard a familiar rumble. He wasn't as into old cars as the Calloways—he drove a three-year-old SUV off the job and it suited him fine—but he'd spent enough time helping them work on their vehicles to recognize the 'Vette's engine.

Balancing on the ladder, he turned to look. The 'Vette was too flashy to miss, especially on a nice day with the top down and two gorgeous women inside. Catching sight of her husband, Anamaria waved that fake beauty-queen-in-a-parade wave, but Ellie, in the passenger seat, didn't seem to notice anything. She was staring off into the distance, her expression somber.

"You hanging out with Sophy tomorrow night?"

Tommy forced his gaze away from the 'Vette and hammered in a nail with enough force to shake the entire framework. "We haven't talked about it."

Everyone on the department would be working, either in

uniform and patrol car or on foot, at the festival. Not that there was ever much trouble, but Tommy was in no position to argue with the chief.

But working didn't mean he couldn't enjoy the festival. He didn't have to actually patrol—just hang out, have a good time and be available if something happened. He could ask Sophy to go with him, have dinner with her, dance with her in the grass around the gazebo.

Or he could go alone, stake out a place in the shadows and watch Ellie as she worked the deli booth.

Admitting which option sounded more appealing was pathetic.

"You can always ask Ellie," Russ said.

Tommy shot him a venomous glare that Russ just shrugged off. "You guys have broken up a half-dozen times, but you always get back together. What are you waiting for? Quit driving everyone nuts and settle this."

"Don't take advice from an idiot," Robbie said. "Remember, this is the man who took six years—and a wife—before getting back together with Jamie."

Russ sent an obscene gesture his brother's way. "So I know what I'm talking about. Six years is a hell of a long time to waste. So is six months."

Tommy finished securing his end of the frame, then climbed down the ladder. Russ was right about that. But getting back together...it just wasn't that easy. Before he'd called it quits with Ellie the last time, he'd talked to his father and grandfather about it. The two men had raised him after his mother left; they were close.

His father had asked one question: *Are you happier with her or without her?* To him, it was that simple. Despite his wife's problems, Phil had been happier with Lilah than without. He would have continued to track her down when she was out drinking and take her home, to overlook her highs and deal with her lows, to take care of her *and* Tommy, to be the responsible one in the family. It wasn't perfect, but it had been better than not knowing where she was, what she was doing, whether she was even alive.

But Pops had understood that Tommy couldn't settle for that. He understood the value of commitment. He'd had the comfort of knowing that Gran had always loved him every bit as much as he'd loved her.

Tommy wasn't sure Lilah had been capable of loving anyone.

Just as he was convinced that Ellie was.

Though he didn't have a clue whether it could be him.

The brothers went on working, bickering as they tended to do. The days were mostly gone when they settled their disputes with punches or smacks. They still stuck together, though. Like ticks on a deer, their granddad Calloway used to say, and Tommy had been lucky enough to be one of those ticks, along with their half brother, Mitch Lassiter.

But they were all married now. Mitch, the second in line, had two daughters, and oldest brother Rick and his wife were expecting a daughter within the month. Russ had Sara Elizabeth, and even baby brother Robbie would soon have Gloriane.

And Tommy couldn't settle for what Ellie was willing to give, and didn't want what any other woman might give.

It was a hell of a place to be in.

They finished the last booth shortly before five. It was up to the participants to decorate them in time for the 6:00 p.m. start of the festival Saturday evening. Last year he'd helped hang crepe paper and streamers from the deli's booth and had learned the fine art of fake spiderwebs. Boiling cauldrons had lined the counter, and the staff, dressed as wicked—or wicked-sexy—witches, had put a nicely ghoulish touch on things. And after the festival—

Shaking away the memories, Tommy helped pack away the tools and load them into the bed of a Calloway Construction truck. Russ headed home to see his wife and daughter, and Robbie left, too, planning to meet up with Anamaria for an early dinner at the country club with Sara and Jack.

Tommy picked up a scrap of lumber they'd overlooked and tossed it in a trash can, then hesitated. It was barely a block in one direction to Sophy's shop, a little less in the other to his SUV in Robbie's office lot. He could ask Sophy to have dinner with him, or eat alone and watch the History Channel—probably the same plans both his dad and Pops had for the evening.

Or he could…how had Russ put it? *Settle this* with Ellie. Literally, *settle*. For less than he wanted, less than he needed.

He was lonely, but he wasn't desperate. Yet.

Still, as he walked along the sidewalk toward River Road, something just steered him into a right turn through the gate that led to the deli. Something kept him moving along the path, up the steps and across the porch. Just hunger, he told himself as he stepped inside. A craving for a bowl of their prize-winning potato-broccoli-cheese soup and a roast beef sandwich on fresh-baked bread.

Carmen was leaning against the wall, talking with two other servers. The early birds would start arriving within the next half hour, followed by the usual Friday evening crowd, but for the moment business was slow. She pushed away from the wall and met him near the glass counter that displayed an assortment of cheesecakes and pies. "She's in her office," she said without a greeting.

He blinked. For the better part of five years, it had been routine for him to come in most nights, for Carmen to say, "She's in her office," or the kitchen or the bar, and for him to go wherever. Six months, and the comment had still been second nature for her.

He hesitated before saying, "I, uh, want an order to go."

Carmen flushed as she pulled an order pad from her apron pocket. "Oh. Yeah, sure."

He rattled off his order, adding a slice of carrot cake, and Carmen went to the kitchen. Aware of the other waitresses watching him and whispering, Tommy shoved his hands in his pockets and turned to study a painting on the wall.

A moment later, he felt the change in the air as the two waitresses left the dining room. His nerves damn near humming, Tommy crossed to the broad hallway that led to the bar, the kitchen and the rear dining room. The aroma of barbecue drifted on the air as he kept walking to the end of the hall where a window looked out on the kitchen garden. He could see Ellie's VW Beetle in the parking lot beyond, a flash of lime-green directly beneath the one pole light.

He turned back restlessly, retracing his steps. When he came even with the oak door marked Office, he stopped, went on, then pivoted and returned. He was standing just inches from the door, knowing it would be stupid to knock, clenching his hand at his side to keep from doing it anyway, when her voice carried through the wood.

"Hi, this is Ellie Chase again. Would you please ask Mr. Aiken to call me as soon as he can? He has my numbers. Please tell him that it's really—" a sound interrupted, sort of a choked cough, and her voice lowered "—really important. Thanks."

He continued to stare at the door after the phone call ended. Who was Mr. Aiken, and what was important enough to bring that stressed tone to her voice?

Whatever the answers, there was one simple truth: it was none of his business.

Scowling, he walked away from the door.

"Halloween is trouble enough at home," Carmen grumbled. "I don't know why we have to make more work for ourselves at work."

Ellie ignored her friend's grumbling. Carmen was a complainer by nature, and having five kids didn't help. Easter, the Fourth of July, Thanksgiving and Christmas were all trouble enough at home, according to her. She didn't realize how lucky she was to have those kids and a home and a husband, and Ellie knew if she pointed it out, Carmen would snort and say, *Take one of 'em, or two or all of 'em—please.*

It was two o'clock on a sunny Saturday afternoon, only four hours from the trick-or-treat parade for candy that would kick off the festival. One of the waitresses was in the deli, filling huge plastic cauldrons with so much candy that it would take two people to move them to the porch, and everyone else who could be spared from waiting on the usual Saturday customers was helping out in the kitchen or with the booth.

Which was coming along very nicely. Ellie stepped back a few feet to survey their efforts. The plywood frame was enclosed with black vinyl, orange streamers fluttering from the top and from the counter that ran along two sides. Spiderwebs, with large black spiders anchored on them, stretched from corner to corner, and fake tombstones leaned precariously against the posts. Large glass jars lined the short end of the counter, filled with fake eyeballs, ghostly-looking fingers and hands and a decapitated head that was ghastly green, its white hair floating gently in the liquid inside.

Eww. Ellie liked it.

"Reliving your childhood, I see."

Stiffening, she slowly turned to Martha, standing a few yards away with a foam cup from A Cuppa Joe in hand.

"My childhood?" she repeated. "You mean, the House of Horrors?"

"Poor thing. You had it so tough, didn't you? At least in your version of things. The truth of it was, your life was pretty cushy."

Ellie checked to see if anyone was near enough to hear, but Carmen and the others had returned to the deli. "Cushy?" she repeated incredulously.

"You had a roof over your head, food to eat and clothes on your back. What more could a kid ask for?"

"Gee, I don't know. Support. Trust. Affection. God forbid, maybe a little love."

Typical of Martha, she focused on only part of Ellie's answer. "Trust? You mean believing your lies? Ignoring when you got into trouble? Ignoring what the police and everyone said about you?"

"I told you the truth."

Martha shrugged as if disagreeing about nothing more important than the weather. "You lied. You whined. You complained. You were an ungrateful brat who was never satisfied with everything your father and I did for you."

Ellie stared at her before shaking her head in disbelief. Martha had always been good at rewriting history. Oliver hadn't cared enough to argue with her, and with little family and few friends to disagree, her version of events usually stood.

When it became clear that Ellie wasn't going to rise to the bait, Martha sipped the coffee. Today she wore jeans and a short-sleeved plaid cotton shirt with worn loafers. Her hair was combed and sprayed into place, and she'd even made a stab at applying makeup. To anyone who didn't know her, she looked respectable, normal, like any other middle-aged woman in town.

But Ellie knew too well that there had never been anything respectable or normal about Martha.

"Have you given my proposition any thought?"

I haven't thought of anything else. But Ellie kept the words to herself.

"You really don't have a choice. You've got too much to lose here." Opening her arms wide, Martha turned to encompass the square and, symbolically, the entire town. "These people won't even bother to spit on you when they find out the truth. They won't come to eat at your fancy restaurant. They won't want you at their merchants' association meetings. It'll change the way they feel about you. They might say it won't, but trust me, it will. They'll think less of you. They won't want you anymore."

Martha knew how to push Ellie's buttons, knew her insecurities and fears. Hell, she'd created most of them herself. She'd made Ellie feel unworthy, had told her over and over how little she had to offer anyone.

And Ellie had always believed her.

She wanted to argue with her now, to insist that her friends and customers would stand by her. She wanted to believe it herself, but the only person who'd ever stood by her in any way was Randolph Aiken, and his support had grown out of his job.

She'd tried to call him the day before, leaving two messages with his voice mail before finally getting a call back from his assistant. Randolph was on vacation in Europe, Marie Jensen had said, and wouldn't be back for nearly a month. She would be happy to pass along Ellie's message the next time he checked in, probably in a week or so.

Too late.

Though, Ellie reflected darkly, it had really been too late from the moment Martha remembered she had a daughter out there somewhere who might have something to lose.

"I'm not asking for a lot," Martha went on. "Put my name on the deed to the house and on the restaurant papers. Give me keys to both of them and your car. Move my stuff into your house. Oh, yeah, and the money." She looked at Ellie, and her lower lip curled in a sneer. "It's no more than I deserve for the life I gave you."

"If you got what you deserved, you'd be rotting in hell right now alongside your husband," Ellie ground out. Her chest was tight, and she couldn't draw enough air to ease the panicked feeling streaking through her. Giving up ownership, even half, of her house and business, having to face Martha every morning and night, listening to her complaints and lies…

It's no more than I deserve for the life I gave you.

When she was fifteen and desperate, she had begged her parents for the chance to live with them again. Dear God, now she couldn't bear it. She *wouldn't*. It was no more than she deserved for the person she'd become.

"Are you asking for an answer now?" Ellie was so numb inside that everything felt frozen, her lips barely able to move to form the words.

"It would be nice. But I'm paid up at the Jasmine for a few more days, and those two gay guys do know how to spoil their guests." Martha drained the last of her drink and tossed the cup toward the nearest trash can. It hit the rim and bounced to the ground.

"I'll tell you what, Beth. Pastor Fitzgerald and his wife are picking me up in the morning for church. You can give me a ride home, and we'll shake hands on it then. Then you can have a day or two to get the house ready for me. Since I've already paid for the Jasmine, I might as well enjoy the whole bit. When my money runs out there, you can move me into your house." Her smile was ugly. "*Our* house. We'll be together again, just like a family."

Never. By the time church was dismissed the next day, Ellie would be hours away. She would head west, maybe to California or Washington or even Alaska. She would go someplace where Martha would never find her, would change her name and appearance and accent so that anyone who did find her wouldn't know her.

A sick calm descended over Ellie. She didn't want to run away, but it was the only realistic choice.

Numbly she walked to the trash can, picked up the coffee cup and dropped it inside before facing Martha again. "All right. Tomorrow, then."

Despite her earlier certainty—*You really don't have a choice*—surprise darted across Martha's face. Had she thought Ellie would be more stubborn? Had some truly malicious part of her hoped Ellie would refuse so Martha could share her secrets with everyone in town?

"All right," she echoed after a moment. "See you then, sweet daughter."

Not if I see you first.

"Oh, look, there's my new friend, Louise." Martha stretched onto her toes to wave at Louise Wetherby, coming out of the flower shop across the street. Louise was active in all aspects of the community and, as owner of the steak house a few blocks away, one of Ellie's biggest competitors.

"Louise, let me help you with that," Martha called, starting toward her. A few yards away, she turned back and grinned at Ellie. "Later, little girl."

Ellie watched her cross the street and take an armload of flowers from Louise. Then she sought out Carmen, returning from the deli with an armload of foam cups. "I've got to run a few errands. Do you mind?"

"You're the boss. Just be back here by six. Don't leave me alone with the little hooligans."

"I won't." Instead of cutting through the restaurant, where someone would surely stop her with some question or problem, she circled around the building, climbed into her car and drove away. Her first stop was the bank, where she made a substantial withdrawal from the ATM.

Her second stop was home. The house was quiet and exactly as she'd left it that morning. She tried to imagine Martha living there, but everything inside her cringed away from the thought.

In the bedroom—the back room, the one Martha wanted for herself—Ellie pulled two suitcases from the closet and began filling them with clothes. It was methodic work: pull garment from hanger, shake out, fold neatly, place in suitcase. She concentrated on it, refusing to let unwanted thoughts into her mind, like where she would go, what she would do, how she would live.

She packed her clothes, shoes and makeup. She dumped her toiletries into a canvas tote bag and her personal papers, along with an inexpensive photo album, into another; then she walked slowly through the house.

Two suitcases and two tote bags. Not much to show for thirty years. But the last time she'd been homeless thanks to Martha, she'd had far less: the clothes on her back and a great terror. Now she knew the worst that could happen; she'd lived through it. Now she had money and job skills. She knew how to take care of herself.

Her thoughts went to the photo album in the bag. Pictures of Tommy, Robbie, Russ and Jamie. Holidays with the Mariccis and the Calloways, day trips from the nursing home with Pops Maricci. Short vacations she and Tommy had taken together.

She'd never had friends to leave behind. How was she going to stand that?

The same way she'd stood getting arrested at fifteen when her supposed best friend slipped her drugs into Ellie's purse. The same way she'd stood those days in jail, finding out her parents had thrown her out, learning how to survive on the streets of Atlanta, doing what it took to survive.

She was strong. She would turn off her emotions. She would get through it by sheer force of will. She would leave here, find a new place, start a new life.

And she would never be vulnerable to anyone again as long as she lived.

Chapter 4

"Why aren't you in costume?"

Tommy looked at Anamaria, gorgeous in a lemon-yellow top, a bright African-print skirt that swirled around her ankles, a shawl in another print that should have clashed but didn't and enough flashy jewelry to add twenty pounds to her pregnant-but-slender frame. "Where's Robbie?"

"Gone to find me some hot cocoa. Where's your costume?"

"I'm dressed as a detective for the Copper Lake Police Department."

She scowled at his jeans, polo shirt and leather jacket. "That's how you dress every day."

"As a detective. This is my costume."

She made another face. "Have you seen Ellie?"

Tommy ignored the tightening in his gut. "I assume she's somewhere over there." He gestured in the direction of the deli and its booth. He'd been at the square since before six o'clock;

it was now seven forty-five, and he hadn't yet made it to that corner. There had been no need. There'd been no trouble, the food was just as good at this end and the music could be heard all over.

"Have you seen Sophy?"

Tommy shrugged. He'd run into her and Kiki a while earlier, both dressed like something out of the *Arabian Nights*. Kiki had hinted that he and Sophy should dance, and he'd deliberately ignored the hints until finally they'd moved on, Kiki in a huff, Sophy quieter. Of course, Sophy was always quieter than Kiki—so was a cement mixer—but this had been in a bad way.

He didn't want to hurt her, lead her on or take advantage of her. He liked her, he really did, but he wished he'd never asked her out.

When Anamaria started to open her mouth again, Tommy beat her to it. "When Robbie gets back, why don't you two go dance while he can still get his arms around you?"

She tossed her black curls, looking regally, primitively fierce. "Ha. We can still do a lot more than dance."

"Yeah, but you're like a sister to me. I don't want to hear about it."

Unexpectedly, she laid her palm against his cheek. "That's the sweetest thing you ever said to me." Then the touch turned into a sharp tap. "Go see Ellie. Talk to her. Tell her you've been a fool."

Because he didn't want to admit how often he wanted to do just that, he scowled at her. "Why?"

Taking his hand, Anamaria studied his palm a moment, drawing her fingers featherlight over the lines there. "Because you belong together. She's your future. You're hers. The sooner you two accept that—"

He drew his hand away. "You're preaching to the choir, Anamaria. I'm the one who wanted to get married, have kids and spend the rest of our lives together, remember? She's the one who didn't." It hurt to say it aloud, but some things were supposed to hurt for a while. If they didn't, there was a problem.

Anamaria's expression turned sad. "I wish I understood why."

"You and me both." He gestured. "Here comes Robbie."

His buddy was dressed in khaki cargo pants, a plaid shirt, an olive-drab vest and a khaki fishing hat, with both vest and hat covered with lures. Tommy recognized the hat and vest as belonging to Granddad Calloway, who'd taught them both the fine art of fishing when they were five or six years old. Robbie hadn't put on a costume of any sort since the year they were fifteen, so this must have been Anamaria's doing. The things a man would do for the woman he loved…

Anamaria was smiling at her husband in a way that made Tommy feel like a pervert for watching. They were the least likely match he'd ever known: an illegitimate mixed-race fortune-teller and a lazy, white, shallow, aristocratic Southern lawyer. Stranger, even, than Robbie's brother Rick, a special agent with the Georgia Bureau of Investigation, and his wife, whom he'd met while she was dancing in the strip club where he was working undercover.

But Robbie and Anamaria *were* a match, and for the long-term. Tommy loved them—she really was like a sister to him, and Robbie had been his best bud all their lives—but he envied them.

Suddenly too restless to stand still, Tommy took a few steps back. "I'm going to take a walk around. I'll catch you guys later."

He shoved his hands into his pockets and headed toward River's Edge. The farther he got from the square, the fewer people he saw, mostly families carrying worn-out kids to their cars.

At the end of the block, he turned right. Ahead a woman with two young boys were headed to their car. Both boys were dressed as ghouls, and they were chanting in unison. "Trick or treat, smell my feet, give me something good to eat."

Once they got in the car and drove away, the street was so quiet Tommy could hear the buzz of the streetlights. The music sounded more than a block away; so did the murmur of the crowd. He felt a hell of a lot more than a block away. He should cut out—he was only obligated to stay two hours. He should take some sweets and visit Pops at the nursing home. Every holiday had been important in Pops's life—all the big ones, plus Halloween, Labor Day, Washington's and Lincoln's birthdays, back when they'd been holidays—and he always got nostalgic, telling stories that Tommy had heard so many times he could tell them himself. Still, he always liked hearing them again. He liked that glimpse into the past, when Pops was younger and healthier, when Gran had been alive, when his dad was happier and his mother hadn't yet lost herself in a bottle.

He turned right at River Road, walking back toward the square. As he reached it, a group of hooligans and goblins darted around him on both sides. One of them called back an apology, and Tommy grinned. He and the Calloway boys had been hooligans for real when they were growing up, but Sara had seen to it that, by God, they were polite hooligans. They were fast on the trouble, even faster on the apologies, and had always managed to sound sincere. Usually they even had been. They'd never meant to cause trouble. They'd just wanted to have fun.

Once the kids were past, his gaze went automatically to Ellie's booth, well lit to show off its creep factor. There were two women behind the counter, plus another one waiting on customers at the handful of small tables set up around the booth. All three women were in costume: wenches all, in low-cut, off-the-shoulder blouses and long skirts, with wigs and scarves. The shorter, rounder one was easily identified as Carmen. He wasn't sure who the other two were, but he did know neither was Ellie. He would recognize her even if she was covered head to toe and wearing a full-face mask.

Dodging a couple dancing in the street, he stepped onto the sidewalk that ran in front of the deli and, as if she'd been summoned by his thoughts, found himself a half-dozen strides behind Ellie. She wore a costume similar to her waitresses: a white blouse, ruffled sleeves pushed off her shoulders, a black skirt with a long slit, a brightly printed scarf tied around her waist to emphasize the curve of her hips and soft black boots. With a black scarf tied around her head like a do-rag taming the wig, the red curls exploded once free of the fabric, electric and wild and surprisingly sexy.

A couple of quick steps and he could be beside her, could say, *Hey, how are you? You look great, want to spend the night with me?*

I miss you, I want to see you again, even if you don't love or need me.

I'm happier with you than without you, so I'm giving up—pride, hope, the future.

Instead of speeding up, he slowed his steps.

Ellie turned through the gate at the deli and was halfway to the steps when something made her stop short. Turning sharply, she headed toward the side of the building. Entering the restaurant through the kitchen? Avoiding diners she'd have to see if she used the front entrance?

Not his concern. As she'd told him before, not much about her was anymore.

He expected to see her disappear around the back. Instead, she stopped about midpoint, arms folded across her chest, spine straight, radiating tension. A shorter, stockier figure faced her from a few feet away.

Martha Dempsey wasn't in costume. She wore jeans and run-down loafers, and a plaid shirt collar stuck up over the neck of a black and orange sweatshirt. She held a foam cup in one hand, a cigarette in the other.

Curious, Tommy moved into the shadows of a tall evergreen azalea, one of a half dozen he and Ellie had planted themselves a few years earlier.

"—agreed to meet after church tomorrow," Ellie was saying, her voice cold. He'd been on the receiving end of that icy disdain a few times himself. It wasn't a pleasant experience.

Martha swayed unsteadily. "You might as well get used to having me around, Ms. Ellen Chase, 'cause we're gonna be a family again."

"We were never a family." More ice, more disdain, accompanied by anger.

Oblivious of the emotions, Martha gulped from her cup. "I'm gonna like living here in Copper Lake. Everybody's so friendly and welcoming. And you…well, you're just gonna make it all that much better, aren't you?"

Ellie glared, the light from the streetlamp leaching color from her. Her face was pale, as unyielding as stone, and her breathing was shallow, tight. Tommy had seen her angry, aroused, amused, hot and warm and cold, but never quite so passionate. Whatever was between her and Martha threatened her composure, as if she might lose control for the first time in the five years he'd known her.

"I wish to God you were dead." Her voice was strained, taut with emotion.

Strong sentiment, but Martha's response was a sly smile. "But I'm not dead. I've got a good twenty-five years left, and I'm gonna spend them with you."

Even from a distance, Tommy could feel the emotion ratcheting through Ellie. Her fingers tightened into fists, and she opened her mouth as if to argue, clamped it shut and breathed deeply before speaking again. "I agreed to meet you tomorrow after church. Until then, get the hell off my property and stay the hell away from me."

Quick as a snake striking, Martha's hand shot out and smacked sharply against Ellie's cheek. Tommy was stunned, more so, it seemed, than Ellie. He left the shadows, covering the distance between them in a few strides. "What's going on here?" he demanded.

Martha's smile was smug and phony. "Nothing, Detective. We were just having a little conversation."

"Are you all right, Ellie?" He studied her in the colorless light. Her cheek was mottled, her eyes frigid and glittery. A muscle twitched in her jaw before her lips turned up in the faintest of smiles.

"I'm fine." But her voice was distant, her expression detached.

"Like I said, Detective," Martha butted in, "we were just talking."

Tommy kept his attention on Ellie. He wanted to wrap his arms around her, to offer her comfort that he knew she wouldn't accept. He settled for moving to stand between her and Martha. "Do you want to file charges against her? I'd be happy to take her in."

"Charges?" Martha repeated, outraged. "For what?"

"Assault. Public drunkenness. Trespassing."

"That wasn't an assault, was it, Ellie? I just gave her a little pat on the cheek. And I'm not drunk." Martha grinned crookedly. "Believe me, I've been drunk before. I know the feeling. I've just had a little sip or two to keep me warm. And as for the trespassing, I'm sure Ellie would disagree with you on that, too. We were just talking. No harm, was there, Ellie?"

Tommy shifted his gaze. "Ellie?"

For a moment she looked as if she'd disappeared somewhere inside herself; then she gave a little shake of her head. "No harm," she agreed tonelessly. "Martha's just leaving. I'd appreciate it if you'd escort her back to the square."

Before he could protest, Ellie walked off toward the alley.

He turned back to scowl at Martha. "What the hell is going on between you two?"

She stabbed one finger in his direction. "You are entirely too suspicious. Ellie and I are old acquaintances starting a new friendship. Now, are you going to do like she said and escort me back to the square?"

"I'd rather throw your ass in jail," he muttered under his breath as he gestured for her to lead the way to the street.

She heard him, though. "I'm sure you would. But you know what, Detective? You and me are going to be friends."

Yeah, right. And Ellie was going to show up at his door after the restaurant closed, wearing that sexy off-the-shoulder blouse and the red wig and asking him to take both off.

Hell, he'd do damn near anything to make that happen.

Even become friends with Martha Dempsey.

Trembling, Ellie stopped in the shadows outside the restaurant's back door. Her hands were shaking, and her chest hurt from the panic that had wrapped itself around her. She should get in her car and leave right now. Her bags were loaded. She had everything she was taking with her. She could call the deli before abandoning her cell phone—she didn't want friends calling once they realized she was gone, didn't want something as simple as a GPS chip in a phone to track her down. She could tell the staff she had a headache, or was tired, or Halloweened-out. They would close up for her. They would tell her to go home, rest, take care of herself, that they would see her on Monday.

And by Monday she would be hundreds of miles away.

But when she moved, she went to the door, not the car. She let herself in, passed the storeroom and walked through the kitchen, smiling automatically at employees, not slowing until she reached the bar.

She wasn't a drinker; growing up with parents who were could turn a kid off alcohol forever. But it was her last night in the restaurant, her last night in town, and she'd never even had a drink in her own bar. Her cheek was throbbing—memory, not lingering pain—and she was feeling…too much. Too hurt, too angry, too scared, too bitter, too alone.

She stopped at the bar, and Deryl Markham came over. He grinned, looking too young to even be in a bar, much less tending one. "Name your poison, boss."

"What's hot?"

"The cider."

She thought of the alcohol-and-cider smell coming off Martha, and her nose wrinkled.

"Cocoa," Deryl went on. "The pumpkin spice ale is ice-cold but selling hot."

"I'll have that. I'll be over there." She nodded toward a booth in the corner, sat down, closed her eyes and began rubbing her temples. Her muscles ached from too much stress, and she didn't expect them to relax any time soon.

"Ahem."

Opening her eyes, she found an unfamiliar witch standing beside her table, glass in hand. She set it down, then slid it toward Ellie. "The waitresses are busy, so I offered to deliver this for Deryl."

"Thank you."

The woman started to leave, then turned back. "You look like you could use some company. Mind if I join you?"

I could use a new life, a new past, a new future. But no company. But Ellie forced a smile and gestured toward the other bench.

The witch detoured to the bar and picked up her own drink, then slid onto the bench. Her costume was no cheap one-time-only outfit. The black robes were heavy, made of substantive fabric, and her hat bore no resemblance to the cheap, floppy things Ellie and the female staff had worn last year. Her hair, coarse strands of black heavily mixed with gray, was either real or a good-quality wig, and her makeup job, complete with

warts, was outstanding. She could have been a regular at the
diner, a neighbor or the woman who shared her church pew
each Sunday, and Ellie wouldn't have a clue.

"This town certainly knows how to celebrate," the witch said
with a careless wave around the room. An ornate ring of braided
silver on her right hand glinted in the light.

Ellie glanced around. Deryl was dressed in an Atlanta Braves
baseball uniform, and the few other customers were also
costumed. "They enjoy it."

"It's great for the parents. All the fun of Halloween with
none of the risks." The woman's voice was soft, definitely
Southern, but unfamiliar. If Ellie had met her before, it hadn't
been consequential enough to remember.

Smiling politely and wishing she'd taken the drink to her
office, Ellie picked up the glass and sipped. It was cold, fragrant
with cinnamon and cloves and allspice, but that didn't hide the
fact that it was ale. Bitter and far too strong a reminder of Martha.

Still, she took another drink. If it would soothe her nerves
and ease the pounding in her head, she would even drink the
icky liquid the green head was floating in at the booth.

Feeling a bit of warmth with the second, longer drink, she
focused on the witch. "Do you live in Copper Lake?" People
from cities thought a town of twenty thousand was so small that
everyone knew everybody else—probably true for Tommy and
Robbie, but not most people. She had her small group of
friends, acquaintances, fellow church members and business
associates, and recognized some other folks, but the majority
of people in town remained strangers to her.

"No, I'm visiting a friend. I don't know where she's gotten
off to. We agreed to meet at the bandstand at nine, so I thought
I'd warm up with a drink until then. I'm from Augusta."

"Nice city." Ellie took another drink and realized the glass
was half-empty. Was she feeling better? In some ways. Her

teeth weren't grinding anymore, and she was pretty sure her head wasn't going to explode, after all. In fact, she was starting to feel a little drowsy.

She realized the witch was speaking again, though her voice seemed to come from farther away than just across the table, and Ellie had to concentrate on listening.

"—should be going. My friend's always early, so I don't want to give her time to get herself in trouble." The witch slid to her feet, her robes rustling around her, and gave an incongruous wink. "At least, not without me." In a voice reminiscent of *The Wizard of Oz,* she added, "Finish your drink, my pretty, then go find yourself a handsome rogue and enjoy the rest of the evening."

"I will," Ellie said, saluting her with the glass. She wished she could take the woman's advice. Wished there was a handsome man in her life. Wished there was *any* man in her life.

No, she didn't, she amended as she watched the witch leave, then took another swallow. Men had been the source of much of her heartache. There had been too many, starting with her father and ending with Tommy. But it wasn't fair to lump Tommy in with the others. He was a good guy, possibly only the second she'd ever met. All he'd ever wanted was her—for her to trust him, love him, marry him, have babies with him.

She couldn't.

No matter how much she wanted it, too.

Suddenly unbearably tired, Ellie got to her feet, swaying a bit. She set the glass down, then her retreating fingers spilled it onto its side, ale splashing her skirt, puddling on the table. Grimacing, she swallowed the last bit, then headed for the bar. "Can I get a towel, Deryl? I spilled my drink over there."

"I'll get it, boss," he replied, and she gratefully nodded.

Her office was far enough away from the front of the restaurant to mute the sounds of the ongoing celebration. The air was warm inside, smelling of the potpourri in a dish on her desk, and the space was dark. Welcoming. She reached for the light switch beside the door but missed, her hand brushing brick instead. She was so tired…

Ellie pushed the door shut, leaning against it for a moment, rubbing her cheek. When Tommy had intervened outside and she'd realized that he'd witnessed Martha slapping her—hardly the first time, but for damn sure the last—she'd been filled with shame and anger and hatred. *I wish to God you were dead,* she'd said, and she'd meant it.

God help her, she really meant it.

Footsteps sounded in the hallway outside the door. Staff, customers—she neither knew nor cared. Carefully she straightened and found her legs unsteady. The pumpkin spice ale should come with a warning: hazardous to your balance. She took a few cautious steps to reach the couch, sat down, then slowly stretched out on the cushions. She didn't have time to waste—so much to do, so many miles to put between herself and Copper Lake and Tommy—but her ears felt as if they were filled with cotton, her body seemed heavy as stone and even in the near darkness, her vision was blurry. She should have known that ale, stress and a lack of drinking experience weren't a good combination.

Just a rest. That was all she needed. A brief nap, time to recover, and after that she could…

After that she…

She would do something, she thought as she drifted off. She just had to remember what.

Tommy escorted Martha Dempsey back to the sidewalk and to the far end of the block. Mostly, that meant holding on to her arm to keep her upright. She practically ran into a light pole and apologized profusely to the metal before he dragged her aside; then she began humming along with the band, a tuneless sound that drove him nuts in three seconds flat.

"What's between you and Ellie?" he asked, as much because he wanted to know as to stop that damned noise.

Martha smiled goofily at him. "Ask me no questions and I'll tell you no lies."

"You make a habit of lying to cops?"

"We all have our lies and secrets. Me, you, Ms. Ellen Chase."

"Why did you slap her?"

"I didn't."

"I saw you."

Martha's head lolled to the side and she squinted to bring him into focus. "That was just a little pat on the cheek, like I told you. Like she told you."

All Ellie had said was that she was fine, which she wasn't. That there'd been no harm done, which there had been.

Tommy would give a lot to know everything about her and Martha, but she wasn't talking, and neither was Martha.

"What are your secrets?" he asked, guiding her around a cluster of kids comparing the takes in their trick-or-treat bags.

"If I told you that, then they wouldn't be secrets." She smiled, flirtatious in a creepy way. "You tell me one of yours and I'll tell you one of mine."

"How do you know Ellie?"

"That's no secret. We've been family for years."

"Funny. She was pretty adamant back there that you were never family. Were you involved with her father?"

Martha stared at him a moment, then started laughing. Quickly the laugh turned into a hoarse cough that ended in a sputter, and her gaze narrowed. "Did she tell you that?"

He didn't answer.

"Well, there's family, and then there's *family*. And there's *involved* and involved. You'd have to ask her to be more specific."

When they started to turn onto Oglethorpe Avenue toward the bed-and-breakfast, she pulled free, swayed and leaned against the stop sign for support. "Thanks for the escort, Detective, but I'm going that way." She nodded toward the couples dancing in the street and, on the edges, the folding chairs that flanked them. Robbie and Anamaria were out there; so were Russ and Jamie and Sarah and Jack Greyson.

And Sophy. With Joe Saldana.

He wasn't surprised, and sure as hell not jealous. Mostly... relieved.

"No, you're not." Tommy whistled sharply, catching the attention of two officers across the street. When he beckoned, Pete Petrovski jogged over to join them. "Give her a ride, will you? She's got two choices—the Jasmine or the jail until she sobers up. No place else."

Pete nodded. "This way, ma'am—"

Martha clasped both hands around the stop sign post and glared at Tommy. "You don't want to arrest me. For Ellie's sake."

He doubted Ellie could care less whether Martha spent a few hours in a cell. Unless she meant she would somehow make Ellie regret it.

And then *he* would have to make Martha regret ever coming to Copper Lake.

"It's your choice," he said with a shrug. "Sober up in a cell or in your luxury room at the Jasmine."

She straightened the best she could, drawing her shoulders back and leveling a disagreeable gaze on him. "I choose the Jasmine."

"I thought you would." He nodded to Petrovski, and the younger officer took Martha's arm and led her across the street to his patrol unit.

Tommy watched until the taillights disappeared in the night, then walked half a block north before turning down the alley. He didn't kid himself that he was going straight to his car, that he would resist the temptation to go into the deli. He needed to check on Ellie.

Needed to see that she was all right.

Needed to let her know that he was there if she needed him.

Yeah, right.

He reached the gravel parking lot behind the deli, barely large enough for five vehicles, and stopped. Ellie's usual space, the one directly underneath the only light, was empty. She was already gone.

A drive past her house proved a waste of time. No car in the driveway, no lights on besides the porch light. Her best friends in town were Anamaria and Jamie, who were both still at the festival, so she couldn't have gone to see them, and she for damn sure hadn't gone looking for *him*.

She probably was fine, just as she'd said.

Though he'd never felt less *fine* himself as he drove home to spend the rest of the night alone.

The pounding in Ellie's head woke her from a sound, if restless, sleep. She tried to roll over in the bed and practically fell to the floor, shoving one hand out to catch herself. Puzzled, she opened one eye, squinting, then the other.

She was on the sofa in her office and, judging by the dim light leaking in around the blinds at the window, had spent the night there. Her mouth was dry and her tongue felt twice its size. Her body ached as if she'd lain in the same position all night, and her head was throbbing, pounding.

No, the pounding came from elsewhere, loud enough to make her wince, distant enough that telling where it originated was impossible.

"All right," she said impatiently, but the words came out as little more than a mumble. Even that small movement of her jaw forming two indistinct syllables was enough to make her stomach turn, but she gritted her teeth and forced herself to slowly sit up.

The room danced before her, the distortion reminding her of a fun-house mirror. What had she done last night? She'd worked at the booth in the square, pretended to have a good time, had a run-in with Martha, seen Tommy and then…

She couldn't remember. But her mouth tasted like sweat socks, and she still wore her wench's costume, even the curly red wig. Had she gotten drunk? Was this misery a hangover?

Gritting her teeth, she pushed to her feet and swayed unsteadily. "Dear God, make this go away and I won't do it again, I promise," she whispered, but once again the words lacked voice.

Pulling the wig off and clutching it by a handful of curls, she stepped out into the restaurant. Sunday was the one day the deli was closed, and it seemed strange to have the sun up and the kitchen empty. Strange for her to be there. Stranger still because she was supposed to be somewhere else, doing something else, something important. She just couldn't remember what.

The pounding was an insistent knock at the back door. She headed into the kitchen, the sound growing louder and more difficult to bear with each step. At last her fingers, stiff as if she'd slept with them knotted all night, twisted the lock, and she pulled the door open.

Tommy stood on the stoop, wearing jeans and a T-shirt, his jaw unshaven and his hair on end. A few feet behind him was Kiki Isaacs, fellow detective and best friend to Sophy Marchand. Ellie never had cared much for Kiki, and certainly didn't want to see her when she was feeling so whipped.

"Where the hell have you been?" Tommy demanded. "I've been knocking for nearly ten minutes."

She leaned against the doorjamb for support. "I have a headache." The words came out this time, though hoarse and raspy.

"A hangover is more like it," Kiki muttered.

"We need to talk to you." Tommy moved forward a step.

He looked more serious than Ellie had ever seen him, and worried, too.

She glanced past him to what she could see of the parking lot. The Charger was there, parked at the foot of the steps, and a police car was behind it. When she looked back at him, she noticed the badge clipped to his belt.

Kiki, the Charger, the badge—he was working. This was an official police visit. Something had happened. Something bad that somehow involved her. But what? She hadn't gone anywhere in the last eighteen hours. Hadn't done anything.

Didn't remember anything of the last nine hours.

Numbly she stepped back, moving into the kitchen, stopping to lean against a stainless-steel counter. Tommy rested his hands on the same counter from the other side, and Kiki took up position at the end, between them and the door.

"Did you spend the night here?" Tommy asked.

"I guess so."

"You guess so?" Kiki sounded scornful. "You don't know?"

Ellie looked at her a moment, then turned her attention back to Tommy. "Why? What's going on?"

"After I saw you last night, where did you go?"

Her eyes closed briefly as she tried to remember. She'd been on her way from the booth into the restaurant when Martha had called her into the side yard. They'd talked, Martha had slapped her and Tommy had stepped out of the shadows. Where had she gone?

"I came in here," she said, opening her eyes again. She'd walked through the kitchen, exchanged smiles with the staff, gone to the bar, talked to Deryl. *What's hot?* she'd asked him, and he'd replied, *The cider.*

She hadn't ordered cider, she was sure of that. Even fermented apple juice couldn't match the bad taste in her mouth or cause the throb in her temples.

"Did you go anywhere else?"

I'll be over there, she'd told Deryl. A table in the bar? A booth? With a drink much more potent than cider. After all, she couldn't have a hangover without a stiff drink first.

But she couldn't remember. Not leaving the bar, not sitting down, not taking a drink. Not going to her office or passing out on the couch. Her memory jumped from *I'll be over there* to Tommy's relentless pounding on the door just moments ago.

Had she gone anywhere?

"I don't—I don't remember. What is this about?"

"Those are the same clothes you had on last night," Kiki said.

Ellie glanced down. The blouse Anamaria had loaned her was wrinkled and smelled faintly of fried onions, stale smoke and liquor. The scarf around her waist was twisted, and the black skirt looked, well, as if she'd slept in it. Her makeup was surely worn off or smudged, her cheek was tender and her hair was flat and limp after so many hours under the wig. Self-consciously she ran her fingers through it, then wiped under each eye with her fingertip. She needed a hot shower, a glass of cold water, a handful of aspirins and clean clothes, not in that order.

Then she needed to get on the road. *That* was the something important she'd forgotten: to put as many miles between her and Copper Lake as she could before anyone realized she was gone. She hadn't even made it out of the damned restaurant. Now she was about eight hours behind schedule.

"No, this is my regular Sunday outfit," she said sarcastically to Kiki. Straightening her shoulders, Ellie started to fold her arms across her middle, realized she was still clenching the wig in her left hand and dropped it on the counter. Both Tommy's and Kiki's gazes went to it, then to each other, and Tommy's expression turned even more somber.

"What's that?" Kiki gestured toward the skirt, and Ellie looked down.

The fabric was cheap, and so was the dye job, the black faded except for a large spot near the hem. "I don't know. It was busy in the booth last night. I must have spilled something."

"What, do you think?" Kiki asked, her tone suspicious and sarcastic and obnoxious all at once. "Let's see…it doesn't look like oil or mustard. Or cider or tea or cocoa or pop. What else did you have in there that you could have spilled?"

"I—I don't know." Ellie rubbed her forehead, wishing the dull throb that had settled there would go away, wishing she could think more clearly. Then she looked past Tommy, out the window behind him, and saw her car, and in the instant it took the sight to sink in, everything inside her went numb.

She was virtually always the last one out of the deli after closing. Though she wasn't afraid of the dark, not anymore, she saw no reason to tempt fate. That was why she always parked in the same space, the one best lit by the streetlamp overhead.

But her car wasn't in that space this morning. Instead, it was pulled carelessly across the two spaces next to her slot.

And there was a dent in the front end. A big one. Marked with something in a dark crimsony shade, like paint or…or…

Horror growing, she glanced at the stain on her skirt again. She gathered a handful of fabric, lifting the hem higher. Whatever had soaked into the material had left it heavy and stiff. Dear God, it wasn't—it couldn't be—

Tommy's voice, sounding far away but still ominous, cut through the buzzing in her ears and fed the panic rising inside her. "Martha Dempsey died last night. It looks like a hit-and-run. Her body was found in the eleven-hundred block of Cypress Creek Road."

The blood drained from Ellie's face, and her hands, her legs, her entire body began to tremble. Oh God, Martha was dead. Her *mother*. The woman she should have loved best but instead had hated most. Killed. Just down the street from

Ellie's house. And there was a dent in Ellie's car, and blood on Ellie's skirt.

Whirling around, she reached the trash can just in time to empty her stomach.

Chapter 5

Tommy dampened a paper towel in the sink, squeezed it, then walked around the island, offering it to Ellie when the retching stopped. She was as pale as the ghosts that had flitted around the square the night before, her brown eyes looking huge and confused and… Was that guilt?

Absolutely not. Whatever had happened to Martha Dempsey, Ellie hadn't been responsible.

Even if she had told the woman *I wish to God you were dead* a few hours earlier.

She accepted the paper towel, wiped her face, then tossed it into the trash can. Her hands were still shaking, and her pulse beat heavily at the base of her throat. "I—I live in the twelve-hundred block of Cypress Creek."

He knew that. Kiki knew it. Presumably Martha Dempsey had known it. Had she gone looking for Ellie to continue the conversation he had interrupted outside? There were no sidewalks in that part of town; the only choices for walking were the uneven grassy shoulder and the street itself. She had likely taken the easier path. And someone had struck her as she staggered in the traffic lane.

Someone, but not Ellie.

Though her car had a dent in it.

Though the dent appeared to have blood on it.

Though her skirt also appeared to be bloodstained.

Not Ellie, he thought again fiercely.

"Someone hit her?" Her voice was weak, unsteady. "Who?"

"If the driver had stuck around to tell us, we'd call it a hit-and-stay instead of a hit-and-run." Kiki all but sneered. "Do you have any clothes here? We're gonna need that outfit."

"I don't...." Ellie shook her head longer than necessary, as if she didn't realize she was doing it.

She was in a hell of a state. Hungover? Probably. Tommy could smell the alcohol on her. Sleeping in her office, still wearing the same clothes... She wasn't a drinker; he'd never seen her take anything more than a celebratory sip or two of wine. But she'd been pretty stressed lately—ever since Martha Dempsey had come to town—and one or two drinks would have a more extreme effect on her than on a woman who was accustomed to liquor.

"We're gonna need your car, too," Kiki went on. "When did you get that dent?"

"I—I don't know. It wasn't there the last time I drove it. Someone must have banged into it in the parking lot last night."

"Banged into it, huh?" Skepticism underlay Kiki's tone. "Banged into it hard enough to spin it around and knock it out of its parking space, and nobody saw or heard or noticed?"

"The car was fine last time I drove it," Ellie insisted.

"When was that?"

She rubbed her forehead again. "I don't— Yesterday afternoon, I think. I went home between, I don't know, two and three. Then I came straight back here, and..."

"And?" Kiki prodded. "You didn't go anywhere else?"

"No." Ellie sounded sure—or was it desperate? Then her voice softened. "I don't think so. I don't remember."

Tommy extended his hand, palm out, in Ellie's direction. "Don't say anything else."

Predictably Kiki puffed up, scowling at him. "Hey, Maricci, this is an investigation into a suspicious death. If she's got nothing to hide, then she should want to answer our questions."

Ellie's gaze shifted rapidly between the two of them, back and forth. She looked as if she wanted to say something, but apparently she decided to take his advice. She kept her mouth shut.

"Do you have anything to hide, Ellie?" Kiki asked pointedly.

Arms folded over her chest, Ellie didn't say anything, but lowered her gaze to the floor.

"I'd like to speak with you outside, Detective." Kiki's voice had turned cold as ice, colder, even, than Ellie's had been the night before when she'd wished Martha dead.

"I'll be out in a minute," he replied.

"You'll come now." Kiki went to the back door and yelled, "Petrovski, get in here!" When Pete trotted up the steps and into the kitchen, she stabbed a finger in Ellie's direction. "Watch her. Don't let her leave your sight."

"Sure thing, Kik—uh, Detective."

One brow arched, Kiki looked at Tommy, then jerked her head toward the door. Ignoring her, he pulled his cell phone from his pocket and held it out to Ellie. "Call Robbie and tell him to get over here now."

Looking sick, she took the phone and fumbled it open.

Tommy followed Kiki outside, closed the door and shoved his hands in his jacket pockets, rocking back on his heels. She stalked down the steps to the gravel lot, paced to the rear of the Charger, then spun around and came back. "What the hell are you doing in there?"

He took the steps slowly, stopping a half-dozen feet from her. "Watch the attitude, Isaacs. I'm still your supervisor."

She snorted. "And what are you teaching me? How to screw up an investigation? All the evidence points to Ellie, and everyone knows how you feel about her. Telling her not to say anything? Advising her to call a lawyer? Damn! You shouldn't even be working this case."

He wouldn't defend what he'd done. If they'd switched places and she was telling someone not to answer his questions, he'd be pissed, too. One call to the lieutenant who headed the detective division or to the chief, and he'd be yanked off this case faster than Kiki could open her mouth.

And that would be fine with him. It would save him the effort of informing the L.T. that he wanted off.

"Damn it, Tommy, she's a suspect!"

"Ellie didn't kill that woman. Not on purpose, not by accident."

"You sure of that? She knew the woman, but they weren't friendly. She lied about leaving the deli last night. Her car has a nice Martha Dempsey–size dent with blood on it. Her dress has what looks like a bloodstain. All she says is 'I don't remember' and 'I don't think so.' And then there's the wig."

Seeing in his mind the tangle of new-penny-copper curls on the stainless counter, Tommy scowled. In the time it had taken to drive from the accident scene—crime scene?—to the deli, he'd tried to remember if he'd seen anyone else last night with a curly red wig. On or off duty, he was pretty observant, and the answer, regretfully, was no. Ellie's was the only synthetic red hair he'd seen in a while.

Except for the single strand that the crime scene tech had lifted from Martha Dempsey's body.

That didn't mean it had come from Ellie's wig. Or that it had fallen there after Martha was run down. It didn't even mean it had gotten there through any doing of Ellie's. The hair had been on Martha's sweatshirt. Maybe when she'd slapped Ellie last night, the hair had caught on her hand, then fallen, landing on the shirt. Maybe she'd swiped her hand across her shirt, depositing it then.

If he voiced those possibilities to Kiki, she would counter with the likelier possibility: the hair had fallen after Ellie had hit Martha with her car, then got out and checked to make sure she was dead or dying. The same time she'd gotten the blood on her skirt.

If it was blood. The lab would have to tell them that.

Deliberately he focused on Kiki's earlier comment rather than the evidence that did, on the surface, lead straight to Ellie. "Okay, Isaacs, this is me teaching. You consider her a suspect?"

"Hell, yes. Any reasonable person would at this point."

"Then why haven't you read her her rights?"

Her gaze narrowed, her mouth thinning.

"Come on, you were questioning her. You were demanding her clothing and her vehicle. What happens when you question a suspect without reading her her rights?" He didn't give her a chance to answer. "A good lawyer sees that none of it makes it into court. You learned that in Cop 101, Kiki."

She shoved at a strand of hair that had fallen over her eyes. "Okay," she said, taking a slow breath. "But we're allowed to interview people about the victim and the circumstances of her death without Mirandizing them."

"Not when you've already tagged them as a suspect in said death. You want to go into court and testify under oath that you didn't consider Ellie a suspect before you questioned her? Because you should know now, I don't perjure myself. Not for you, not for anyone." Not even Ellie. Though if anyone could tempt him to break that rule...

Kiki kicked a piece of gravel that skittered across the lot, then leaned against the Charger. Her lower lip jutted out in a pout. "You're only being so picky because you like her."

"I can make the argument that you're only being so careless because you don't like her. And believe me, if I can make it, Robbie can, too, and he'll be a hell of a lot more persuasive." He glanced up as the sound of a familiar engine came clearly on the thin morning air. "We don't *have* all the evidence yet. We don't have a cause or a time of death. We don't have a motive. We don't even know that getting hit by the car had anything to do with her dying. She could have passed out, hit her head and died before the car struck her. She could have had a heart attack. There are a lot of possibilities, and we're nowhere near ruling them all out."

"We can't lose possible evidence because we don't have enough answers yet."

"Our only risk of losing evidence right now is if you keep bulldozing through this. We're going to do it by the book."

"I don't remember seeing the page in *my* book where it says the lead detective should lawyer up for the suspect," she grumbled as Robbie's Corvette turned into the alley.

Tommy watched Copper Lake's best criminal defense attorney—Ellie's criminal defense attorney; what a weird thought—pull into a nearby space and shut off the engine before he looked at Kiki again. "Tell me you wouldn't do the same for Sophy."

Her only response was a grudging shrug.

Robbie looked as if he'd been dragged out of bed four or five hours too early. He combed his fingers through his hair, then rubbed one hand across his jaw as he approached them. "You know, some of us like to get up at a decent hour."

"You think we wanted to get called out at 5:00 a.m.?" Tommy responded mildly.

"You're up then anyway, except on Saturdays. Where's Ellie?"

"In the kitchen." Tommy wished he could go inside with him, could sit beside Ellie and offer moral support or something. Of course, that wasn't even in the realm of possibility. He, Robbie and Ellie would all have to be fools to allow that, and Robbie, at least, was no fool.

Besides, she didn't want Tommy's support.

Or anything else.

Ellie sat numbly in the back dining room, a bottle of water open in front of her, a croissant untouched on the saucer beside it. She'd talked with Robbie awhile, maybe fifteen minutes, maybe an hour. Nothing seemed real. Time didn't pass, nothing made sense, everything was out of control.

Pete Petrovski stood in the doorway, arms crossed, gazing out the windows that lined the back wall. He'd brought her the water and scrounged around the kitchen until he found the croissant left over from yesterday's breakfast. He'd even offered to go down to A Cuppa Joe's for her just before Robbie had arrived and sent him away with nothing more than a look.

Now Pete was back, and Robbie was outside, talking to Tommy and Kiki. She didn't move, though. She wasn't sure her legs would support her.

Martha was dead. Ellie was stunned, yes, but not sorry. The emotion churning inside her was for herself. Had Martha's threat to reveal her past died with the woman, or would it all come out anyway? As long as her death remained a police matter, Ellie wasn't safe. They would look into Martha's background, gather her belongings from the bed-and-breakfast. They would find the originals of the files Martha had given to her Wednesday night, and they would figure out that she'd been attempting to blackmail Ellie.

One more reason to consider her a killer.

Dear God, *had* she done it? Had she left the deli last night, run down her mother in the street and left her there to die? Was she capable of that kind of desperate act, that kind of rage?

She didn't want to believe it. There had to be another explanation. Her mother, her car, her past, her clothes, but someone else was guilty.

Even she didn't buy it.

The back door closed, and then a moment later, Tommy, Robbie and Kiki came into the dining room. Kiki pulled a garment from the canvas bag she carried and shook it out, then nodded to Ellie. "Come on. We need your clothes."

"Anamaria sent a dress for you," Robbie said in explanation. Probably a maternity dress, since Ellie hadn't been long and lean like her in a lot of years.

It took monumental effort to get to her feet, then follow Kiki to the women's bathroom. When she would have gone into a stall, the woman stopped her. "Change out here."

The police want to take my clothes and my car, Ellie had said on the phone. *Robbie, they think I killed someone!*

They'd discussed Kiki's request when he arrived, and he'd advised her to cooperate. If she didn't voluntarily turn over the costume and the car, the police would just get a warrant. It would prolong the process, but in the end, the result would be the same: either way, she was giving up both clothes and car before she left here.

The dress Anamaria had sent was grass-green, a simple sheath, stopping short of the knees, the sleeves ending above the elbows. She stripped off the peasant blouse, the scarf and the skirt, handed them to Kiki, then tugged the soft cotton over her head.

She looked ragged in the mirrors above the sinks. Her hair stuck out every which way, her eye makeup was smudged and a bruise darkened her cheek. Nothing new there. Last night hadn't been the first time Martha slapped her.

But it was the last.

"Is that where she hit you?"

Her gaze shifted in the mirror to meet Kiki's, and she nodded mutely. Tommy had told her about it, had also, no doubt, told her that Ellie had wished Martha dead mere hours before she was killed. No wonder, with everything else, that Kiki looked at her as if she'd already been convicted.

No wonder Tommy had stopped the questioning and told her to call Robbie. Bless him for that.

Running her hands under cold water, she managed to bring some order to her hair. Kiki gave her another minute to wipe away some makeup with a damp paper towel, and then they left the bathroom. Kiki went into the kitchen with the costume; Ellie returned to the back dining room. Through the window, she saw a couple of people in the parking lot, examining her car. They wore T-shirts marked CSU on the back, and they were looking for evidence that she was a killer.

Shuddering, she sat down, Tommy to her left at the small table, Robbie to the right.

Tommy broke the silence. "How did you know Martha Dempsey?"

Tell the truth, Robbie had advised. Getting caught in a lie, especially one that didn't relate directly to Martha's death, would just make the cops wonder what else she was lying about.

Easy for him to say when he didn't know the truth. *She's my mother.* Truth. *My selfish, hateful, abusive mother who threw me out of the house when I was fifteen for something I didn't do.* Motive.

"I knew her growing up," she said, staring outside though she couldn't see the activity in the parking lot.

"In Charleston?"

"Atlanta." She felt his gaze intensify. Yes, she'd lied about that. She'd lied about so many things. If she stopped now, all

the untruths would collapse and bury her beneath their weight…
or send her to prison.

"Was she a neighbor, a teacher, the church organist?" The
tension that sharpened his voice radiated in the air, as well, raw
and edgy against her skin. "Was she involved with your father?"

"Yes." True, as far as it went.

"And he's dead."

"Yes." Completely true, and a relief. If she weren't so
worried about being blamed for Martha's death, if she weren't
wondering whether she was guilty, she would feel nothing but
relief over it, too. Giddy, free-from-the-past relief.

"Last night you said you'd agreed to meet her after church
today. About what?"

"She wanted to talk. To relive old times." Oh God, she didn't
want to tell any more lies. She wanted to grab hold of Tommy,
tell him she couldn't remember the night before, that she didn't
know if she'd killed Martha. She wanted to cling to him, lean
on him and let him make everything all right. That was what
he did, after all—served, protected and made people feel safe.

"And you didn't want to."

"I don't like talking about the past." Finally she faced him
head-on, for the first time since he'd given her his cell phone.
He looked tired, as if he hadn't gotten more than a few hours'
sleep, and the expression in his dark eyes was grim. Beard
stubbled his jaw, and the way his mouth was set, she would bet
he was really wishing he hadn't given up smoking last year.
Don't feel you have to do this for me, she'd said after one par-
ticularly testy day, and he'd grinned, looping his arm around
her waist and drawing her near.

*I'm doing it for me. When we start having kids, I don't want
to be outrun by a two-year-old.*

Her throat constricted, and a tear or two pricked at her
eyelids. No kids for her. No marriage. Even if she ran away,

even now that Martha wasn't alive to follow and threaten her, she would still have to get Tommy out of her system before she could even think about another man, and that wasn't likely to happen. Some broken hearts were permanent.

Did he see something in her face, or was that deepening scowl his typical expression for interviewing murder suspects?

"How much did you have to drink last night?"

"I don't know. I guess too much."

"Who was working the bar?"

"Deryl." What would Deryl tell him? That she'd gotten bombed, announced she was going to kill someone, then staggered out of the bar? Or that she'd had only one drink for courage before leaving the bar, that when she'd returned, there had been blood on her skirt and her car was banged up, that she'd gotten bombed then to forget?

"Who else did you talk to last night besides Deryl?" Tommy asked.

"I don't remember anyone." Lifting one hand, she kneaded the taut muscles in the right side of her neck. "After running into—" Bad choice of words. "After seeing you and Martha, I wanted a drink. I've never had a drink in my own bar. So I came in through the kitchen, I went to the bar and I...had several drinks. Too many."

"I thought you didn't know how many," he reminded her, his expression impassive.

"Look at me!" she snapped. "I look like I've been run over—" Horrible choice of words, shuddering through her with revulsion. "Like I've been through the wringer. I stink of booze. I smell it, I taste it. I slept on the couch in my office in those awful clothes and that awful wig, my head is throbbing and I'm seriously thinking about puking up my guts again. Does that sound like too many drinks to you?"

"Yeah. It sounds like about ten times more alcohol than I've seen you drink in the five years you've lived here. Why last night? What was it about Martha that made you decide it was a good time to get drunk?"

Chilled, Ellie hugged her arms to her chest. "I didn't decide. I just wanted a drink." One drink, to take the edge off the tension that had been screaming through her. She was pretty sure she hadn't even intended to finish it. Just a few sips, to get warm, to relax a bit, to get the nerve to climb into the car and leave. Flee.

Just one drink. But it must have done such a great job of taking the edge off that she'd ordered another. Surely even a nondrinker like her couldn't get stinking drunk and pass out from just one drink.

Abruptly Tommy took another tack. "Martha said that she had a good twenty-five years left and she was planning to spend them with you. She said you were going to be a family again."

There wasn't a question in there, but Ellie shook her head. It never would have happened. First she would have run the hell away from Georgia. She'd taken money from the bank, her bags were packed and in the car—

Her gaze jerked once more to the rear windows. They were going over her car with a fine-tooth comb. They would find the suitcases. Soon they'd find out about the bank withdrawal, and they would discover Martha's blackmail material at the Jasmine. Motive upon motive.

Kiki came around the corner into the dining room and took the seat across from Ellie. Her manner was bristly, her expression almost blank, but smugness eased in around the edges. "What do you say, Ellie? Want to go to jail today?"

Ellie and Kiki had never been friends, but things had gotten worse since Tommy had started dating Sophy. Kiki, it seemed, thought Ellie was standing in the way of her best friend's happiness, because Tommy had been in love with her.

She'd never wanted him to love her. Sex was easy, dating

was easy. But needing, loving, committing… She had too many secrets. Too little trust. Too little faith in herself, in him, in anyone's ability to see what she'd been, to know what she'd done, and want to know her anyway.

She didn't want to know her.

"What do you have, Kiki?" Robbie asked.

"Preliminary tests show it is blood on both the skirt and the car. Of course, the lab will have to tell us it's Martha Dempsey's. The crime scene guys found some clothing fibers caught in the crumpled metal around the bumper. I'm sure the lab will also identify those as belonging to Martha Dempsey, as well. And, hey, the car was packed up. Like you intended to leave town in a hurry, Ellie."

Tommy and Robbie both swiveled around to stare at her, Tommy's dark eyes filled with hurt, Robbie's blue gaze with smoldering anger. She wanted to apologize to them, but she was too stunned by the first part of Kiki's announcement. That was definitely blood on her car, on her skirt. She'd curled up on the couch in her office and slept the night through with her mother's blood soaking into her skirt.

Oh God.

Lurching to her feet, she dashed to the bathroom and shoved the door open hard enough to make it bounce. Kiki's "Hey!" sounded distant, along with the scrape of a chair and heavier footsteps coming her way. Her stomach heaved, sending blood rushing through her ears, blocking out the steps, and her vision turned blurry as the retching started again.

When it stopped, she leaned weakly against the stall wall. She knew it was Tommy waiting on the other side of the thin partition, though he hadn't spoken, hadn't come any closer than the bathroom door. She could hear it in his breathing, could feel it in the air, in her own taut muscles.

I'm good at waiting, he'd told her the first time he'd

proposed to her, the first time she'd turned him down. *One of these days, you'll change your mind, and I'll be here.* She'd never changed her mind, but he'd always been there.

She wished he would leave, not just the bathroom but the restaurant. She wished he didn't have to see her this way, looking like death warmed over, smelling that way, too, vomiting, giving lousy answers to important questions, suspected of killing someone. She wished she could preserve a little dignity. She didn't have much, but she needed it.

But he wasn't going anywhere, and the god-awful taste in her mouth left her no choice but to leave the stall. She flushed the toilet, then opened the door, keeping her eyes downcast as she washed her hands and rinsed her mouth with water scooped from the tap.

"You were leaving." His voice was soft, his tone not dismayed or disappointed, but disillusioned. "Without saying goodbye. And you weren't coming back."

And finally she had no choice but to face him. The lie was there, ready to come out—*I needed a break. Just a few days. Charleston or Savannah or Beaufort. I would have been back later in the week.* But all she did was nod.

It was as if something in him snapped. He advanced on her, backing her against the wall, not touching her but holding her there all the same, his body mere inches from hers, his hands on the wall on either side of her head, his face bent to hers. "Why?" he demanded, the question all the more fierce for its low, insistent tone. "Because of Martha? Who was she, Ellie? What did she want from you? Where were you going? What about us?"

She took a breath, painful, shallow, and whispered, "There is no 'us.'"

He didn't move. The distance between them, small as it was, remained the same, but somehow he *seemed* closer, looming, but not threatening. "What about Anamaria, Jamie,

Sara? Robbie and Russ and Carmen? What about your friends, Ellie? Don't you owe them better than that? Don't they at least deserve a goodbye?"

She was so raw inside that even the faint shake of her head sent pain throbbing through her. "I—I couldn't…"

"So you were just going to run away. Disappear. Give up everything you've got here and leave us to wonder the rest of our lives what the hell happened to you." Now he sounded disappointed, and bitterness added its own flavor. The look he gave her was scornful, disgusted, as he moved away.

He walked partway to the door, then returned, staring into her face. "Did you run down Martha Dempsey?"

It was a logical question. He should have asked it sooner. She had asked it of herself, and it terrified her that she didn't know the answer.

But it hurt coming from him. The emptiness in his eyes. The hard set of his mouth. The utter stillness that damn near radiated from him.

"I don't know." Her answer was barely audible—soft, frightened.

He stared at her a moment longer, the muscles in his jaw clenching. Then he walked away.

She watched him go, the door swinging shut behind him with a *whoosh;* then her legs gave out. Sliding down the cool tile of the wall, she sat on the floor, knees drawn to her chest, and imagined she still heard his footsteps. Down the hall. Into the kitchen. Past the storeroom. Out the rear door. Down the steps. She imagined he'd left her for good this time.

I'll be here, he'd said.

Not any longer.

Before he reached the dining room, Tommy made a left turn and cut through the kitchen to the back door. He took the steps two at a time, then stopped suddenly as he came face-to-face with the crime scene techs, overseeing the loading of Ellie's car onto a roll-back wrecker. They would take it to the police garage, where they would process it. Everything they found would be sent to the lab, where they would say yes, the blood belonged to Martha Dempsey; yes, the fibers came from her clothes; yes, this was the vehicle used to kill her; yes, Ellie Chase was their prime suspect.

The winch on the wrecker whined as it pulled the Beetle into place. Jarred into motion again, Tommy stalked across the gravel to the Charger, unlocking the door with the press of a button, rummaging through the console and the glove box. He found what he was looking for, a crumpled cigarette pack, under the vehicle manual in the glove box.

Tossing the pack and a book of matches onto the old porch that served as a loading dock, he lifted himself onto the ledge to sit before removing the sole cigarette from the pack, then studied it. It was the last cigarette in the last pack he'd bought. At first, he'd kept it around for an emergency, for those usually-late-at-night moments when he found himself alone and feeling weak. But other exertions had filled in nicely: a hundred push-ups, a quick run along the river, making love to Ellie.

Then he'd kept it as a talisman of sorts. It was right there, at hand during the day and easy to retrieve at night, so the fact that he hadn't reached for it all these months proved that he'd really given up the habit for good.

Yeah, right. Proved that you don't know what the hell an emergency is.

He slid the cigarette into his mouth, opened the matchbook and tore off one match. It came away easily and lit on the first strike. Surprising, since his hands were trembling and his lungs felt as if he'd just finished a hundred-mile fun run. He watched until the heat started to sear his fingertips, dropped the match to the ground and tore off another.

Robbie came out of the restaurant as the wrecker slowly pulled out of the parking lot with Ellie's car. The crime scene techs were right behind it. He came to lean against the loading dock next to Tommy. "Jesus."

Since there was nothing Tommy could add to that, he didn't try. Instead, he lit the second match, the flame barely able to flicker thanks to his unsteadiness.

"You need help with that?"

"I've been lighting my own cigarettes since we were fifteen and stealing them from your granddad."

"Yeah, but your hands don't usually shake like that."

Tommy dropped the second match, and it landed on a chunk of gravel, extinguishing itself an instant later. "She was planning to run away. She wasn't going to tell anyone. She wasn't going to say goodbye to anyone. She was just…going."

The way his mother had. One day she'd been there and life had been normal—as normal as Lilah's life ever got—and the next she was gone. No one knew where she'd gone. No one knew why. He'd spent most of his life wondering if she was alive or dead, if she'd married again, had more children, if she'd ever missed the son she'd left without so much as a hug.

Ellie owed her friends better than that, he'd told her. She owed *him* better. It would have killed him, finding out that she'd just vanished. That he truly meant so little to her that she could walk away without a word. He would have spent the rest of his life searching for her, even if she didn't want him to find her, because God help him, he couldn't have lived without knowing whether she was dead or alive. Whether she'd found someone else. Whether she'd missed him.

"So what's the plan?"

Tommy took the cigarette from his mouth, studied it again for a time, then began methodically destroying it. Robbie had represented suspects in Tommy's cases before. Copper Lake was small; there weren't that many detectives or criminal defense lawyers. Conflict of interest had never been a problem for either of them before, regardless of the outcome. Work was work.

Except when it wasn't. He couldn't imagine anything less personal than this case.

"The plan," he said after a moment, "is up to Isaacs and the lieutenant and the D.A.'s office."

"You're not going to work the case?"

Gather evidence and information that could result in sending Ellie to prison for the rest of her life? No way. Not even if he knew beyond a doubt that she was guilty.

She didn't even know if she was guilty. *I don't know,* she'd whispered, and he'd heard the fear, seen it in her eyes. She'd been so intoxicated that she didn't remember if she'd gotten in her car, driven home and killed a woman in the street.

He'd never been that drunk, not once. But his mother had. Robbie had. No doubt Martha Dempsey had.

"Isaacs will want to confirm that the blood belongs to that woman," Robbie said, leaning against the porch, ankles crossed, with that nine-mile stare he got when they were out on the river, the sun was shining and the fish weren't biting. "There's also the question of fingerprints on the car, on the steering wheel and the door handle. If there are any besides Ellie's…" He trailed off, probably silently running down a list of things to prove or disprove.

Kiki would also have to talk to the bartender, the waitstaff and any diners who might have seen Ellie in the restaurant or bar the night before. The medical examiner would determine the time and cause of death, the lab would process the fibers from the car and try to match the curly red hair to the wig and Isaacs would collect Martha's belongings from the bed-and-breakfast.

Then she, and whoever the lieutenant assigned to work with her, would go sifting through Ellie's and Martha's pasts, looking for a motive.

In Atlanta, not Charleston, where she'd told him she grew up.

What else had she lied to him about?

Robbie glanced at him. "She didn't deliberately kill that woman."

"No," Tommy agreed.

But accidentally? How could he say no when Ellie herself couldn't?

The ringing of his cell phone broke the heavy silence that had settled. He pulled it from his pocket, glanced at caller ID, then flipped it open. "This is Maricci."

"Where are you?" It was A. J. Decker, the lieutenant in charge of the detective division, usually grumpy, always short and to the point.

"Outside Ellie's Deli."

"Where is she?"

"Inside with Isaacs."

"You can't work this case."

"I know. But Kiki can't work it alone." She'd just made detective a few weeks earlier; she lacked the experience to handle a suspicious death on her own.

"I'll be there in five. Tell Calloway he can go back to bed. We won't be arresting his client today. But she'd damn well better not plan on going anywhere." Decker ended the call before Tommy could respond.

"How'd he know I'm here?" Robbie asked.

Tommy shrugged.

Decker knew everything, or, at least, way more than he should.

"If she tries to run off again…"

His jaw tightened and Tommy ground his teeth. "I'll go home with her."

Robbie gave him an are-you-crazy? look. Exactly what he was wondering himself. Seeing Ellie under the best of circumstances these days was tough enough. Babysitting her while she was a suspect in, at the very least, a felony hit-and-run or, at worst, a homicide was going to make that look like a day at the beach.

"If she'll let you," Robbie said after a while.

"You can tell her it's not her choice. If she wants your help, then it's got to be by your rules."

"And what is Decker going to say when he finds out you're moving into her house? You may be off the case, but you're still a cop."

"I can be a cop on vacation. Or, hell, I could not be a cop at all. Russ has always said he'd give me a job."

The surprise in Robbie's expression was nothing, Tommy would bet, compared to what he was feeling himself. The only two things he'd ever wanted to be jobwise were a cop and a retired cop. Nothing else had ever held even the slightest appeal, certainly not construction work.

Without commenting on the idea that Tommy would even consider quitting the police department because of Ellie, Robbie said cynically, "Yeah, but he'd make you work."

It was a family joke that Tommy and Robbie had skated by their entire lives without exerting themselves over anything. Today it didn't seem funny. Nothing did.

"There's Decker," Tommy said with a nod toward the alley and the black pickup turning in. "I'll talk to him. You go warn Ellie."

Chapter 6

Ellie was exhausted and daydreaming about bed and aspirins and quiet when Tommy and Robbie returned to the dining room. No, she corrected with a glance over her shoulder. Tommy, Robbie and A. J. Decker. He was older than the other two men, a few inches shorter, broader in the shoulders. His hair was brown, his features average and his expression always unreadable. He should have been forgettable, but there was something about him, some sense of authority, of *knowing,* that made him the opposite.

And just the sight of him made Kiki Isaacs flinch. Ellie liked him better for that.

He greeted Ellie with a nod and a polite murmur of her name, then asked Kiki to step outside with him. He gestured for Pete to follow, leaving Ellie alone, she supposed, so she and Robbie could speak in private.

But Tommy didn't go with them.

Robbie sat down at Ellie's table while Tommy stood on the other side of the room. "They're not going to arrest you right now."

She exhaled, and thought that must be what it felt like for a balloon to deflate. Tension whooshed out—not all of it, by any means, but enough to make her suddenly feel limp.

"Here are the rules, though. Number one. If you even think of leaving town, I'll turn you over to Kiki before you can finish the thought. Okay?"

She nodded, though truthfully she wasn't ruling out the idea. Thanks to Martha, damn her soul, every ugly detail of Ellie's life was going to come out. There was nothing she could do to stop it. But she could be gone when it happened. She could avoid the looks on everyone's faces, the shock, the little snubs as they inevitably turned away from her.

"Second," Robbie went on, "to make sure you cooperate with rule one, you're getting a roommate. You've already tried to run once. We're not taking a chance on it happening again."

Roommate. Nice way of saying *guard*. Worse than that, another way of saying *Tommy*. The knot in her gut told her; a look at him confirmed it. Numbly she realized she was shaking her head. "N-no," she finally said. "I don't want— I won't—"

"It's not an option, Ellie. If you want my help, you've got to do what I say."

Wonderful. It would be like old times. Except that they weren't friends. They weren't dating. They weren't having great sex. They couldn't even carry a conversation.

But he was still a cop, and she was a suspect in Martha's death. She'd never be able to let down her guard around him.

Not that she'd been able to anyway for the past six months.

She found her voice again, stronger this time, cooler. "Won't A.J. frown on that?"

"I'm on vacation starting today," Tommy replied. "He doesn't much care what I do."

Invite Tommy into her home for the next however many days or weeks. She would rather go to jail.

Liar. She'd been to jail too many times. Fingerprinted, photographed, strip-searched and locked in a cell like an animal. She'd been pepper-sprayed and restrained, and had a few up-close-and-personal run-ins with some scary inmates. Up-close-and-painful. She had sworn the last time that she would never go back.

Resigned to company for the foreseeable future, she looked grimly at Robbie. "Can I go home soon?"

"Yeah, Decker said go ahead."

Instantly, she pushed the chair back and got to her feet, then rested one hand on the tabletop for balance. The queasiness was fading, replaced now by hunger. The best she could recall, she hadn't eaten dinner last night.

A stupid thing to think about, when Martha was dead.

"If he asks questions…" Her gaze on Robbie, she tilted her head in Tommy's direction.

Robbie's grin was halfhearted. "You mean *when,* don't you? He's curious as hell about everything, you know." The grin faded. "Answer them. Truthfully."

How nice that he felt the need to add that last bit. Before this morning, he and Tommy had both believed she was a truthful person: honest, honorable, normal. They were about to find out just how many times she had lied to them. Lied to everyone. Even herself.

"He's on our side," Robbie said as he also stood.

Tommy didn't say anything in his defense. He didn't need to. Ellie could trust him. She'd always been able to trust him. He really was an honest and honorable person. He would do his best to help her, to make sure she really was innocent—or really was guilty, in which case he would do the honest, honorable thing and turn her in.

No. If she really was responsible for Martha's death, she would turn herself in.

"Can we go?" she asked quietly in his direction. Peripherally, she saw him step back and gesture toward the kitchen.

Outside, Kiki and A.J. were talking. She didn't look happy that her suspect was walking away without handcuffs; he was impossible to read, as usual.

Ellie breathed deeply before walking down the steps. Her car was gone. Good. She never wanted to see it, or the dent in the hood, or the blood staining the lime-green paint, again.

Robbie patted her arm, said, "I'll call you," then got in his own car.

Ellie slid into the passenger seat of the Charger, fastened the seat belt, then closed her eyes. Home. Aspirin. Bed. If she could sleep, maybe the nightmare would end when she awakened. She would find out that she'd really tied one on, that it was all liquor-induced, that Martha was alive and well and planning to destroy her and she was still free to run away where no one would ever find her again.

Then Tommy got in beside her and started the engine, and he looked so somber that there was no doubt this was one nightmare she couldn't wake up from.

Just drive, she silently urged, and he did, turning down the alley, then onto Oglethorpe. A moment later, they passed the Jasmine, and Ellie stared at the mansion. Had the police claimed Martha's belongings yet? Had they found the originals of the papers she'd given Ellie, or were they back in Atlanta? Had Martha brought anything else with her that might connect the two of them?

Like what? A family photograph? Ellie couldn't remember ever having one taken. A sentimental keepsake, a drawing Ellie had done for her as a child, her favorite stuffed animal when she was little, a lock of her baby-fine hair?

Martha didn't have—hadn't had a sentimental bone in her body. Any drawings Ellie had done had earned a grunt and a toss toward the trash can. The day they'd thrown her out, they'd also thrown out all her belongings—clothes, books, the thread-bare teddy that had sat on her bed. If there'd been any souvenirs of her infancy or childhood, they'd gone, too.

One day she'd had a home and a sorry excuse for a family, and the next day she'd had nothing but the clothes she wore.

They took the long way home—by a whole two or three minutes—turning onto Thurmond Lane, following it to the end and making a sharp left onto Cypress Creek.

Every muscle and nerve in her body tightened again as she got out of the Charger. Instead of going into the house, she walked to the end of the driveway and stared off to the west, looking for sign of the—the accident? Murder?

"There aren't any skid marks." Tommy stopped beside her, six feet of pavement separating them, his own gaze directed down the street. "There was some blood, but the fire department washed it away when we were done."

"Where?"

He pointed to a spot halfway between her driveway and the neighbor's. On these last few blocks of Cypress Creek, houses were widely spaced; the distance was two hundred feet or more. Not far enough.

"Who found her?" Her voice sounded too normal to be her own. Turmoil inside, and cool control outside. Now that the shaking and the vomiting had stopped.

"Father O'Rourke. He was on his way home after spending the night with one of his parishioners who had emergency surgery."

She knew the priest slightly; he'd often dropped by the nursing home to see Tommy's grandfather while they were visiting, too.

"We don't have a time of death yet, but it was a while before Father O'Rourke came along. Four, maybe five hours. There's not a lot of traffic here late at night."

"No one saw or heard anything." She said it flatly, not as a question, but Tommy shook his head. No one saw her run down Martha in the street. That was good news. But no one saw anyone else do it, either.

Abruptly, she turned and started toward the house. Her little yard was neatly mowed, the flower beds planted just last weekend with purple and yellow pansies. Her house. Her home.

I looked around that pretty little house of yours.

Think about what you stand to lose.

Our house. We'll be together again.

A shudder ripped through her, and she stopped at the foot of the steps. "I can't…" She couldn't stay. Couldn't be in this house that Martha had coveted. Couldn't sleep inside there knowing that someone, maybe her, had run over Martha in the street and left her there like roadkill.

She didn't have to explain it. Tommy shrugged and said, "We can go to my house. Do you want to wait in the car while I pack your stuff?" Then his expression turned dark. "Or is there any stuff left to pack?"

Regretfully she shook her head. She wanted to apologize, to tell him that she'd only been thinking of her own survival, that she hadn't meant to hurt him. But of course he'd been hurt. They'd been together for four and a half years, and he'd spent four of them trying to persuade her to marry him. He loved her, had said so even the day he'd broken up with her for good. He would have been hurt, and she'd known it.

She just hadn't cared.

They returned to the car, and he backed out silently, once again avoiding the accident scene by turning onto Thurmond.

His house was located in the south part of town, halfway

between River Road and the river, only a few minutes from Robbie and Anamaria's condo in distance, but a world apart in status.

The house was on the small side, centered in a compact yard on a street filled with other small houses and compact yards. It had belonged to his grandfather; as Pops had gotten older and more frail, Tommy had moved from his apartment into the room where his father had grown up. He'd done the cooking and the cleaning and made it possible for the old man to live another four or five years in the comfort of his home.

Finally, two years ago, Pops had moved himself into Morningside Nursing Center. It had been harder for Tommy than it had for his grandfather. She'd listened to him rail and argue and blame himself, and she'd held him, just held him, a lot of nights.

She doubted he was any happier with the situation now, even though the nursing home had been a good thing for Pops. He was a sociable man, and there were people to talk to and nurses to flirt with twenty-four hours a day. He was less lonely.

Was Tommy?

None of her business.

He parked in the driveway, next to his SUV, and she climbed out wearily. She gazed at her feet as she followed the cracked sidewalk to the steps, then went into the house. It was quiet in a way that hers never was. The silence in her house was an empty sort of thing. It wasn't a home, just a house where she slept and bathed and, for a time, had sex, but didn't really live.

This house had seen love and laughter, tears, sorrow and joy. It had a sense of *family* about it, of *home,* that she wanted but had never had, could never have.

"You can have Pops's room," Tommy said, closing the door and tossing his keys in a wooden dish on the table next to it. He paused, then picked up the keys again and slid them into his pocket.

He didn't trust her not to steal his car and disappear, she realized, her mouth curving in the thinnest of smiles.

He shouldn't.

He led the way into the hall, then the front bedroom. It was square, with windows on the two outside walls, a ceiling fan overhead and an iron bedstead to which a few flakes of white paint still clung. The bed was made—it was Tommy who'd gotten her into the habit of making her own bed every morning—and covered with an aged quilt. The pillowcases were sturdy white cotton, the edges embroidered with flowers and birds in faded threads.

"Not much has changed since he and Grandma moved in here nearly sixty years ago," he commented, "but it's comfortable."

She nodded.

"I'll call Kiki and see when they'll release your stuff from the car."

There was a nice image: Kiki handling her clothes, checking her sizes, passing judgment on her taste, wondering what Tommy saw in her when he could have Sophy.

"We need to talk," he said, but before Ellie could protest, he moved back into the hall. "After you've rested."

When the door closed, she sank down on the bed and began removing the soft suede boots that looked so wrong with Anamaria's dress. She definitely needed the rest, but she could live without the talking afterward. He had questions she couldn't answer, some because she'd held the secrets too long, others because she simply didn't know.

Such as had she been driving her car when it struck Martha?

Had she done it deliberately?

Dear God, had she murdered her mother?

After wandering through the house four times, Tommy stopped in the bathroom, laying out a new toothbrush and comb, along with clean towels. Back in the living room, he dropped down on the couch, stretched out and shoved a pillow under his head. He turned on the television, but kept the sound muted so it wouldn't disturb Ellie in the next room. There had been a few creaks of the bedsprings, then nothing but silence. She'd looked exhausted. Hangovers could do that to a person.

When he'd told Decker he wanted time off, the lieutenant hadn't even blinked. *You gonna work with Robbie?* He'd had no reaction when Tommy said yes.

Conflicts of interest were different in a small town. Cops investigated people they knew; judges sat on trials involving acquaintances and neighbors. The district attorney would argue a case in court, then have the defense lawyer and his family over for a cookout in the evening. Decker had no problem with one of his detectives trying to prove the innocence of a suspect another of his detectives was trying to nail for a felony.

After all, cops were supposed to build a case against the guilty suspect, not the likely one, not the easy one, and for damn sure not the innocent one.

Which of those was Ellie?

No doubt she had secrets. No doubt she'd lied to him. And if she'd lied about where she was from, she'd probably lied about something else.

Maybe everything. Maybe she wasn't the woman he believed her to be. Maybe he didn't know squat about her—who she was, what she was capable of. Maybe he'd been in love all this time with a total stranger.

He didn't believe it. He couldn't believe it. Okay, so she might have lied about some stuff, but the person she was, deep down inside... He *knew* that person. Knew she was good and sweet and generous and passionate and caring. Knew she would never physically hurt anyone.

He stared at the TV, barely registering the NASCAR race on the screen. *Cars going round and round,* Ellie used to tease. *I'd rather watch fishing.* Fishing hadn't really been her thing, either, certainly not on TV, but kicked back in the boat, face tilted to the sun, a cooling breeze ruffling her hair and a bottle of cold water in her hand... They'd passed more than a few lazy afternoons that way.

Last night's confrontation with Martha, and the meeting they'd scheduled for today, had really upset her. They'd no more been planning to relive old times than Tommy was going to take up with his seventh-grade girlfriend. Another lie from Ellie.

The first thing he and/or Robbie had to do was make her understand that if she kept it up, she would lie herself right into a prison cell.

Ellie in jail. It sounded so ridiculous that he couldn't even form the image.

He had no idea how many laps the cars had made on the silent television when the bedroom door creaked. Ellie came out, barefooted, dress wrinkled, and padded down the hall to the bathroom. A few minutes later, she walked as far as the living room door, her hair combed and her face washed. Still, she looked tired, stunned and hungover. "Are you hungry?" he asked.

She nodded, and he got to his feet, heading to the kitchen. Though his back was to the door, he knew the moment she followed him in. He turned on the oven, then took a pizza from the freezer, handmade the way Pops had taught him. Back in Italy, Pops's family had been in the restaurant business for generations. He might have done the same here in Copper Lake if Grandma had lived long enough to help him.

"How do you feel?" he asked as he peeled off plastic wrap, then set the pizza on a battered pan.

"Like crap."

"Alcohol never makes you feel better."

"I know."

He slid the pan into the oven, set the timer, then turned to face her. She was standing beside the kitchen table, looking vulnerable and ragged.

"My mother was a drunk." Pretty much everyone who knew him knew that, but he and Ellie hadn't talked about it much. It had always been a one-sided conversation, and before long she had changed the subject or, anticipating it, he had. "Lilah drank...I don't know. To ease some pain that no one knew about. To handle her unhappiness. To cope with her depression.

"I have a few vague memories of her smiling and laughing, playing with me, dancing with my dad. But mostly I remember her sitting and staring with a drink in her hand. I could go to bed at night and she'd be sitting on the couch, staring at nothing, and I swear to God, when I got up the next morning, the only thing different was the level of whiskey in the bottle. She always just sat there and looked at things no one else could see, went places in her head that no one else could go."

And then one day, *she* went someplace else. She'd taken her clothes and a photograph of the family, and no one had ever seen her again.

Just as Ellie had intended for no one to ever see her again.

Before the stabbing pain could completely grip him, she sat down and quietly said, "My mother was a drunk, too."

It was momentous—her volunteering something private that not only sounded but *felt* like truth. Still, he opted for cynicism over surprise or being impressed that she'd confided *something*. "The mother you grew up with in Charleston? Or the one you grew up with in Atlanta?"

Her attempt at smiling was phony and a failure. "Okay, now you know the dirty truth. I'm from Atlanta. I lived there until I was eighteen. After that, I settled in Charleston until I came here."

"Why lie about it?"

She shrugged carelessly, another phony effort. "My life in

Atlanta was nothing special. My fantasy life in Charleston made for a better story."

He studied her for a time before turning away to take glasses from the cabinet and ice from the freezer. Her fantasy life hadn't been a better story. It had been normal. Average. The kind of life he and everyone else she knew in Copper Lake could relate to.

Meaning that her real upbringing was something most of them *couldn't* relate to.

After carrying the glasses to the table, he got a pitcher of homemade tea from the refrigerator. Mariccis didn't eat or drink instant anything. He'd brewed it the day before, strong the way he liked it, without sugar the way Ellie liked it. Four-year habits were hard to break, especially when he didn't want to break them.

"Are your parents really dead?" he asked as he poured the tea.

She looked away, and for the second time that day, something like guilt darkened her eyes. "Yes."

"And Martha was connected to them."

"Yes."

"How?"

She wrapped her fingers around the glass, turning it in circles that seemed nervous in spite of their slow control. When it became clear that she wasn't going to answer, instead of pushing, he chose another question. "What made you decide to get drunk last night?"

A question he sensed she felt more comfortable with. "I didn't intend to. I rarely drink. That smell—rum right out of the bottle, beer spilled on the carpet, tequila freshly puked up—that's the strongest memory I have of my childhood. I can hardly remember either of my parents without a cigarette in one hand and booze in the other. It was as natural to them as breathing. I didn't want to be like them."

Some children of alcoholics became alcoholics themselves because it *was* natural to them. Others never went past the first or second drink, because they never got over the revulsion, the anger, the resentment, the fear. Those last few months before his mother left, when he'd found her bottles, he'd poured them down the sink, believing that would make her stop, would make her a better mother. Of course, she'd just bought more.

"Why last night? You're thirty years old. True?"

Cheeks flushed, she nodded.

"You've never been drunk before. You've never even finished a glass of wine before. Why get drunk last night?"

"I didn't mean to," she repeated. "I just wanted a few sips. I was anxious. I thought it would help me relax."

"About meeting Martha today?"

She shook her head, stared hard at the tabletop and murmured, "About leaving."

The buzz of the oven timer gave him an excuse not to respond right away. Using a mitt, he pulled the pan from the oven, then set it on the stove. The crust was thin and crispy, and heavy with toppings: vegetables all over with Canadian bacon on one half, sausage and anchovies on the other. Her favorite and his. Old habits.

After digging through a drawer for the pizza cutter, he tried to make his voice neutral when he asked, "Where were you going?"

"I don't know."

"Were you coming back?"

Her shrug wasn't the fake one she'd given earlier, but a smaller, more vulnerable lift of her shoulders. "Probably not."

"Why?" For this question he turned his back to her, focusing instead on cutting the pizza into neat slices. It was hard enough talking calmly to her about her plan to disappear. He didn't want to watch her consider a lie over the truth, or choose to give no answer at all, as if it weren't important enough to bother. He didn't want to see that she could have run off, leaving the people who loved her sick with worry.

He didn't want to look at her and see his mother.

She was silent a long time, and when she did speak, her voice was unsteady. "Martha brought back a lot of memories that I wanted to stay forgotten. You've probably guessed that my childhood wasn't as idyllic as I portrayed it. I prefer not to remember it. It was another life. I was another person. But she was planning to stay here. Every time I saw her, every time I heard her name or even thought about her…it was easier to leave."

Tommy dished the pizza onto plates. He set one in front of Ellie, the other at his own place, sat down and stared across the table at her. "Easier," he repeated bitterly. "Easier to run out on the people who love you than to deal with a few bad memories? The past is over and done, Ellie. It can't hurt you now."

Her smile was thin. "Spoken like a man who doesn't have a past. Your childhood really was idyllic. You grew up in a nice little town with a father who loved you, a grandfather who adored you, friends, neighbors, everyone cared about you—"

"And a mother who abandoned me. Just like you were planning to. How could my childhood be perfect without her in it?"

"You had plenty of other people in your life."

"I have plenty of other people now, but do you think that makes me miss you any less?"

She stared at him. He knew she wasn't surprised that he still missed her, still wanted her—damn it to hell, still loved her. She knew him far better than he knew her. He had no secrets. What you saw was what you got. It had taken a lot of years for him to fall in love; it would take even more time for him to fall out.

"So you were going to go off someplace where we could never find you, where we could never know if you were even alive, and what? Start all over again? A new life, a new business, new friends, a new man?" He snorted derisively. "Who knows?

You could have ended up next door to my mother. Two weak cowards, living in anonymity, hiding from the only people who give a damn about them."

After a moment, he muttered, "Eat your pizza before it gets cold," and took a big bite of his own. The sauce was hot on his tongue, the anchovies salty, the cheese stringy, and he barely noticed because along with all those other things he still was, he was also still pissed.

Ellie ate cautiously at first, making certain her stomach would tolerate the pie. After two pieces, she picked at the third, scooping the toppings off, breaking off the crispier outer rim and leaving an empty, misshapen crust on the plate. She wiped her fingers on a napkin, drank her tea, then sat back, arms folded across her chest. She looked closed off, detached, and her voice sounded it. "So how does this work? Anything I tell you, you tell Robbie and Kiki?"

He shrugged. He'd never been in this situation before. Robbie, yeah, Tommy would keep him informed. Kiki? He didn't know. Working or not, he was still a cop; if he had knowledge of a crime, he had to share it with the investigating officer. But *anything* Ellie told him?

"I can't answer that until I hear what you're going to say." Of course, that was too late for her if the information was incriminating.

She nodded as if his answer was no more than she'd expected. "This—" she gestured between them "—is a bad idea."

"You'd prefer to bunk down in a jail cell?" Given a chance, she would make a run for it. He was pretty sure of that. Robbie and Anamaria didn't have room for her at the condo; Jamie and Russ couldn't keep a close watch on her; Carmen had too much going on with her husband and five kids. Staying with him might not be her first choice, but it was the only one guaranteed to keep her in town.

Before she could answer, his cell phone rang. He fished it out, saw Kiki's number and considered letting it go to voice mail. Whining or bad news—that was all he'd get from her, and he wasn't up for either at the moment. But, scooping up the last piece of pizza on his plate, he flipped open the phone, left the chair and went to stand at the back door, gazing out into the yard. "This is Maricci."

Behind him a chair scraped, and he shifted just enough to see Ellie carrying their plates to the sink.

"Hey, do me a favor," Kiki said. "Ask my suspect a question for me."

"Yeah, sure, what?"

"What's her name?"

Blankly he bit off a chunk of pizza, then talked around it. "What do you mean? You know—"

"Ellen Leigh Chase is dead. Has been for over fifteen years."

His fingers tightened around the phone, and the pizza suddenly seemed the weight and size of a boulder in his stomach. He dropped the rest of the piece in the trash can in the utility room, then wiped his fingers on his shirt. "There must be—"

"No mistake. Ellen Chase, born thirty years ago in Atlanta, died sixteen years ago in a pile-up on I-20, same city. Then, five years later, same name, same Social Security number, began attending the University of South Carolina, working at a posh restaurant in Charleston, then running a restaurant in Copper Lake." The triumph in Kiki's voice made it more annoying than usual. So did the distrust. "Find out who she is, Tommy, or bring her in. Better yet, forget asking and I'll bring her in. In handcuffs and leg irons."

"You know what you can do with your handcuffs and your leg irons. I'll call you back."

He shut the phone too hard, then turned to look at Ellie. She'd rinsed the dishes and stacked them neatly in the sink, thrown away the dirty napkins and pizza crusts and wiped the counters and the table with a damp cloth. Now she squirted lotion from the bottle beside the sink—her brand, her bottle—into her hands and waited for him to say or do something.

He wanted to believe Kiki was wrong, but running a name and Social Security number was simple enough for a monkey to do. If the computer said the Ellen Leigh Chase belonging to that number was dead, she was dead.

So who the hell was standing in his kitchen? Who the hell had he been in love with all this time?

More lies. Bigger lies.

He'd thought she wasn't capable of murder, but how could he know that when he didn't even know something as simple as her name?

But Martha Dempsey had known. Martha had known her name, her past, all the secrets she'd done such a damn good job of hiding. Martha had been a threat to those secrets, and now she was dead.

Ellie rubbed the last bit of lotion into her skin, then hugged her middle. "I take it that was bad news. Is Kiki on her way to arrest me?"

He began walking toward her, his steps measured, his muscles taut. "She may not have to. I may do it myself." In as conversational a tone as he could manage, he asked, "Who are you?"

She didn't blush like most people. Her cheeks turned a delicate shade of rose that, rather than guilt or embarrassment, damn near screamed out *innocence*. Any rational person would look at her—her blond hair, big brown eyes, that pretty little flush—and know she couldn't possibly have any deep, dark secrets, certainly none that could lead to murder. Any discerning person would trust her in all the things that mattered, and all the things that didn't matter, too.

But she'd been lying since the day she'd come to Copper

Lake. *I'm Ellie Chase*. Her first words to virtually everyone she'd met, including him, had been a lie.

When he came near, she took a step back, continuing to retreat as he advanced. The counter stopped her; she could go no farther, but he kept moving until she was trapped, his prisoner, cabinets at her back, his body in front, his arms at her sides. His face was so close to hers that she blinked, having trouble focusing, but that just made him move a breath closer.

"Ellen Chase is dead," he said in a low, angry voice. "Who in God's name are you?"

Chapter 7

Oh God.

Ellie had dreaded this day for so many years, from the very first time she'd ever said the words: My name is Ellen Chase. She'd been alone with Randolph Aiken that first time, when he'd given her the documentation—birth certificate, driver's license, Social Security card—that changed her from Bethany to Ellen. The real Ellen, he'd told her, was dead. From that moment on, she'd convinced herself that the real Bethany was dead, too.

Tommy was so close, but too angry to touch her. She wished he would. Wished he'd lean his body against hers. Wrap his arms around her. Pull her head onto his shoulder. Tell her everything would be okay because he was there.

But that wasn't going to happen. She had only herself to get through this mess.

And she finally had to share the secrets that had gotten her into it in the first place. Some naive part of her had hoped they would die with Martha, but her realistic side had known that wasn't going to happen. She knew it had only been a matter of time before the police would have found out that Ellie Chase was a liar and a fraud. They would run her fingerprints and discover her real name, her real connection to Martha, her real past. Tommy could hear it from Kiki or from her.

She uncurled one hand from the other and gently touched his arm. He flinched, his muscles knotting, his jaw clenching, and with an inward flinch of her own, she drew back. "Can we talk outside?"

His breathing shallow and controlled, he took a few steps back, then gestured toward the door and the deck beyond.

The wood of the deck was silvered and worn, with wide steps leading down into the yard. Ellie sat down on the top one. The wood was warm against her feet, the sun shining down on her bare arms. Tommy's idea of yard work consisted of mowing. There were no flower beds to soften the edges of the deck, leaves were scattered across the grass and the azaleas that bordered the yard on three sides hadn't been pruned in years. In bloom in the spring, they were a gorgeous sight.

He walked past her to stand in the grass below, hands on his hips, a scowl on his face. "Should I call Robbie for the great reveal?"

His sarcasm hurt, but she hid it. She knew so much more about hiding than revealing.

Of course Robbie would know. Everyone would. By now, she was the latest topic of gossip all over town. Conversations would stop when she came around, or whispers would start. *Did you hear… Do you know… Can you believe…* Then the snubs and the cold shoulders, until one day she would leave town and no one would care.

If Kiki didn't put her in jail first.

"No." This first time, this hardest time, she would tell only

Tommy. Lacing her fingers together tightly in her lap, she said, "Once upon a time—"

"It's not a damn fairy tale," he growled.

No. More like a horror movie.

She nodded and adopted a more fitting somber tone. "I grew up in Atlanta, an only child, in a house on Fairfax Street with my mother and father. They didn't choose to be parents, neither before I was born nor after. I was an accident, and they did the least they could to deal with it."

You had a roof over your head, food to eat and clothes on your back, Martha had pointed out last week. *What more could a kid ask for?*

"My parents weren't strict. They weren't interested enough to be. As long as I didn't cause any problems for them, they didn't care what I did. As I got older, I went to school, I hung out with my best friend, Cheryl, and I did my best to minimize the time I spent at home. My father worked and drank, and my mother stayed home and drank.

"One evening I went to Cheryl's house to study for a mid-semester exam—at least, that was the plan. But she had been invited to a party by her boyfriend, and she persuaded me to go. I didn't even know she *had* a boyfriend."

Smiling faintly, she stared at a thin spot in the grass. She'd thought she and Cheryl shared everything. Her friend was the only one who knew the details of Ellie's life at home; she knew about all the fights Cheryl had with her parents. But she didn't know Cheryl was seeing a twenty-one-year-old man with whom she was having sex on a regular basis.

She'd been so naive.

"Everyone at the party was older. There was a lot of alcohol, a lot of drugs, and a fight broke out. Someone called the police, and when they came, someone slipped some meth into my purse. No one believed me when I said the drugs weren't mine.

We were at a party with all these older people, known drug dealers, everyone with arrest records except Cheryl and me. They looked at where I was and who I was with, and they assumed I was guilty. You know how cops are."

Tommy's tension ratcheted up a notch with the comment.

"I got arrested, the police called my parents and they refused to pick me up. I spent the night in jail, and when I was finally released the next morning, my mother wouldn't let me in the house. By the time I got out of jail, she'd already removed every sign of me from the house—my clothes, my books, the photographs of me. She'd boxed everything up and watched the trash guys haul it off. She told me they'd never wanted a kid, and they damn sure didn't want a kid who got into trouble with the cops. And then she closed and locked the door in my face."

She dared another look at Tommy and saw sympathy in his dark eyes.

"I went to Cheryl's house, but she wouldn't let me in, either, and she couldn't look me in the eye. I finally figured out she was the one who'd stashed the drugs in my purse. I begged her to tell the truth because it was destroying my life, and she said…" Her voice faltered. She'd expected nothing from her parents and hadn't been surprised to get it. But Cheryl had been her best friend. She'd been the one person Ellie had thought would never let her down. "She said, 'Better you than me,' and she went back into the house and just left me there, with nowhere to go, no money, no family, no friends."

It hadn't been the first time she'd been betrayed, or the last, but maybe the worst. She'd never trusted anyone the way she'd trusted Cheryl. Not her parents, not Tommy, not Randolph Aiken or Anamaria or Robbie or Jamie.

But she was trusting Tommy with this story.

Though not by choice.

"I was fifteen, and I was homeless. I slept the first three

nights hidden between the trash cans in the alley behind my parents' house. I shoplifted food and huddled in corners, and my parents lived their lives as if I had never existed. On the fourth day, I tried to get my mother to let me come home, and she threw an empty whiskey bottle at me." Ellie fingered her left temple, imagining she could still feel the split skin and the trickle of blood. "So I moved on. I left our neighborhood—I was too ashamed to see people I knew—and eventually I met other kids who were on their own. They taught me what I needed to survive."

Tommy looked as if he'd turned to stone, a scowl etched into his face, his gaze distant and dark. The only signs of life were the muscle that clenched in his jaw and the faintest movement in his throat when he swallowed. Clearly he'd had no idea what her great reveal was going to be, and just as clearly he didn't like it. He didn't want to hear more. Didn't want to know her secrets, after all.

But now that she had started, she couldn't stop.

"You're a cop, Tommy," she said quietly. "You know what I mean by 'survive.' I snatched purses. I picked pockets. I ran errands for drug dealers. And when none of that was enough, when I got desperate enough, I began having sex with them. With anyone who had the money."

That muscle was so tight that it looked as if it might snap.

She drew a breath, straightened her shoulders and said aloud words she'd never imagined herself saying. "I was a prostitute, Tommy. My real name is Bethany Ann, and Martha Dempsey is—was—my mother."

Tommy was sick.

Not just surprised or stunned, but churning-in-his-stomach, going-to-lose-his-lunch sick. He'd heard lots of sad stories. He knew the god-awful things parents could do to their kids, strong people could do to vulnerable people, but he'd never imagined... He'd never suspected.

Ellie.

Dear God.

His muscles on the verge of spasm from being too taut for too long, he stiffly turned and sank onto the third step, halfway between Ellie and the grass. She was barely a blur in his peripheral vision, but he could hear her shallow breathing. He could feel the tension radiating around her. He could damn near taste the coppery flavor of dread, nervousness, fear.

Ellie, Ellen Leigh Chase, the woman he'd fallen in love with practically the first time he'd seen her, the woman he'd wanted to marry and have kids with and grow old with, was Martha Dempsey's daughter. Bethany Ann Dempsey. Teenage thief and hooker.

If he thought about that too hard, he really would lose his lunch.

He wished she hadn't told him anything. Wished he'd never asked her questions.

Wished he'd never met her.

No. He would never wish her out of his life.

Though he'd wish a different life for her. A different past. One that wasn't so...awful.

"So now you know—" Her voice wobbled, and she drew a sharp breath. "Now you know pretty much everything. I bet you regret asking, don't you?"

He should turn around, look her in the eye and say, *It doesn't matter. It doesn't change anything.*

But it gave her a motive to kill Martha Dempsey. She'd hidden from her past a long time—a new name, a new life, a fantasy upbringing that couldn't have been more normal. If Martha had threatened to reveal everything... Why else would she have come to Copper Lake? Certainly not to make amends. Not out of motherly concern for her only child. She'd wanted something from Ellie—money, most likely; support—and she'd been willing to do whatever was necessary to get it. She'd deserved to die for what she'd done to her fifteen-year-old daughter.

He pictured the woman he'd spent too much time with the past few days—the gray hair, the unhealthy color, the stale stink of cigarettes and booze so pervasive that it had become a part of her. Smug, mean, calculating. Ellie's mother.

Bethany's mother.

The name didn't fit her. She didn't look like a Bethany, didn't feel like one. He couldn't imagine calling her that, or her answering to it. Bethany had died a long time ago, destroyed by indifference and betrayal and abandonment. The woman sitting behind him, waiting for a response from him, could never be as innocent and naive as a Bethany.

Damned if he knew what response to make.

"Please say something, Tommy." Again her voice quavered, a plea from a woman who never pleaded.

He dragged his fingers through his hair, then shook his head. "I need to…" Think. Process it all. Look at it unemotionally, like a cop. Just the facts.

He needed time to absorb that Ellie-he'd-wanted-to-marry was a liar, a fabrication, a desperate kid who'd done desperate things. He had to look at just how desperate those things had gotten.

Did it matter to him that she'd been a prostitute? That the same great-sex stuff she'd done with him, she'd done with other men? *With anyone who had the money.*

Had she killed her mother?

And did that really matter?

Tommy shoved himself to his feet and turned toward her but couldn't quite meet her gaze. "I can't— I really need to—"

He sensed rather than saw her hurt. Damn it to hell, all she needed right now was meaningless words. *It's all right. We'll deal with it.* But he didn't know if anything was all right, if they could deal with anything.

Pivoting, he stalked across the grass and jerked his cell phone from his pocket. Speed-dial number one: Robbie. "Get over here to the house," he said sharply. "I've got to go out, and someone needs to watch—" Instead of saying either name, he hung up.

"Well." The sound was more sigh than word, heavy with disappointment, and he knew he'd officially joined the long line of people who'd let her down.

Easing to her feet as if sudden movement might hurt, Ellie crossed the deck and went back inside the house. A moment later, he followed, hearing snatches of TV shows as she flipped through the channels.

It took Robbie and Anamaria five minutes to get there. Tommy waited in the kitchen, listening for the sound of the Corvette, trying not to hear the echo of Ellie's words. *Please say something, Tommy.*

Anything would have done. *Wow. I'm sorry. That was tough. That's in the past. It's okay.* Like an idiot, he couldn't manage even that.

By the time Robbie and Anamaria reached the steps, Tommy was halfway across the porch. Anamaria's hand brushed his arm as he passed, but he didn't slow. "I'll be back later."

"Hey." Robbie spun around and trailed him to the SUV. "What's going on?"

"I have to go somewhere."

"Where?"

Damned if I know. With a shrug, he climbed into the truck and slammed the door.

Robbie stood in the driveway, scowling at him, as he backed out, then drove away.

After too much aimless wandering, both physical and mental, he found himself sitting in the parking lot of the Morning-side Nursing Center. Pops's room was near the back, but he wouldn't be in there on a day like this. Tommy cut through to the nearest rear exit, then headed for a quiet corner with a table and four chairs in the shade of a maple tree. Pops sat in one of the chairs, his walker to one side, a checkerboard folded up in its box on the table in front of him. He held the Sunday paper on his lap, but he was watching a group of blue-haired women a few yards away instead of reading.

When Tommy slid into the chair to his left, Pops grinned. "That Dorothy Abernathy is quite a looker, even as old as she is."

"She's younger than you are."

"Yeah, but men age better." Pops shifted his gaze to Tommy. "Present company excepted. You look like hell."

"It's been a long day. Where's Dad?"

"Already been here and gone. I whipped him at checkers again." He gestured to the set, then said, "We missed you at church this morning."

"You haven't seen me at church on Sunday in longer than either of us can remember."

Pops shook one bony finger. "Your memory might be failing, but mine is as clear as ever. Father O'Rourke told us about that poor woman. Is that why you've had a long day?"

Poor Martha? Like hell. A better description would be poor excuse for a human being. "Yeah. But I'm off the case."

"Why?"

Tommy leaned back in the chair, exhausted, and it settled an inch or two deeper into the earth. "Because it appears that the prime suspect is Ellie."

Pops snorted in utter dismissal. "Ellie wouldn't hurt a fly."

She'd hurt *him*. To him, it had been so simple: they loved each other. Getting married was the next step, then having kids. Even though she'd never said it, he'd always believed she loved him. The way she looked at him, touched him, smiled at him, made love with him…

But love required trust, and she had none to give.

Pops folded the newspaper and swatted it down on the table. "You *don't* believe Ellie is guilty."

Did he? Martha had thrown her teenage daughter out on the streets, knowing what her options would be for survival. Then, when Ellie not only survived but prospered, she'd hunted her down and threatened her. Ellie had had too much to drink, and those same survival instincts her mother had forced on her might have kicked in. Might have led her to drive home. Might have caused her to flee the accident scene. Might have blacked out the details of the accident.

Or she might be guilty of nothing more than wishing her mother dead.

Leaving the question unanswered, he asked one of his own. "What do you do, Pops, when you find out that everything a person's ever told you is a lie?"

"What kind of lies? Big ones or little ones? Making excuses for things they've done or lying for their own benefit or covering things they're ashamed of?"

Tommy shrugged. Ellie hadn't made excuses. She'd done what she had to to survive, and she hadn't benefitted, unless being treated as a regular person counted. But she was ashamed of the past, or she wouldn't have created the fantasy life with fantasy parents.

Pops's gaze narrowed, and after a moment, his mouth thinned. "Found out something about Ellie you'd rather not know, huh?"

He nodded. Hell, yeah, he preferred thinking that she'd had the fantasy life—a regular home, regular parents who loved her, nothing out of the ordinary. He didn't want to know that she'd been on her own, scared, hungry, homeless, desperate.

"Is this stuff she's done since you met her?"

"No."

"Does it change who you think she is?"

Tilting his head back, Tommy gazed into the branches of the tree overhead. There was just enough breeze to flutter the leaves, to make a soothing rustle that could, and often did on lazy afternoons with Pops, lull a person to sleep.

He'd always thought Ellie was beautiful. Nice. Sweet. Intelligent. Capable. Incredibly sexy. A little guarded. A little distant. Did he think any differently now?

"No. It doesn't change anything." Though now he could add strong and resilient and tough to the list.

"Does it change the way you feel about her?"

He hated that life had been so unfair. He was angry about what her parents and her so-called friend had done to her. It hurt that she'd had to learn so many ugly lessons all at once, and it hurt like hell knowing that she'd lived half her life unable to trust anyone with something as basic as her name.

"No," he said quietly, regretfully. "I still love her. But now I understand why she…" Why she didn't trust him enough to let herself love him back. Why she'd been so willing to give up everything and run away. Why she'd never wanted a commitment, not from him, not to him.

I wish to God you were dead, she'd said to Martha last night. It was fifteen years late in coming, but Martha had finally gotten what she deserved.

"Well?" Pops prodded. "You gonna sit here with an old man all day, or go try to make things right with that pretty girl of yours? You know, I'd like to hold my first great-grandbaby at least once before I die."

Tommy didn't bother pointing out to him that Ellie wasn't his and really never had been. He didn't tell Pops that the odds of them ever having kids were so damn slim that they were nonexistent. They had been from the beginning, but he'd let his hopes blind him.

Was he blinded now?

He knew the past she'd wanted so much to keep hidden. He knew Kiki was determined to make a case against her for Martha's death. He knew she might conceivably be guilty—not of murder, but of hit-and-run. Of driving under the influence, bad judgment and impaired thinking. He knew she would never deliberately take another person's life.

And nothing he knew changed the way he felt. None of it changed what he had to do.

Rising from the chair, he bent and hugged his grandfather. "I've got to go, Pops. I've got to see someone."

Ellie. There was something he had to tell her.

It's all right. We'll deal with it.

Ellie pretended she didn't know to the minute how long Tommy had been gone, but it was a lie. She'd watched television and talked with Robbie and Anamaria, but the entire time a clock had been ticking in her head: one minute, two, five, ten, thirty, sixty.

When a car pulled into the driveway and, a moment later, a door closed, she stiffened. One hundred eighty-eight minutes, give or take a few seconds. It had taken more than three hours for him to decide he could stomach facing her again.

His steps were quiet as he crossed the porch. There were two small thuds; then the door swung open and he came inside, carrying the suitcases and the canvas bags she'd stashed in her car the afternoon before. He set them in the hallway near Pops's room, then stopped in the living room doorway. He didn't look eager to talk to any of them.

"Help me up off this couch," Anamaria said, extending her hand to Robbie. He got to his feet with the natural grace all Calloways shared—one of the perks of good breeding—took her hand and pulled her easily to her feet.

"I'll call you later," Robbie said as he passed Tommy on the way to the front door, squeezing his shoulder.

"I'll call *you* later," Anamaria said to Ellie before her husband tugged her around the corner.

An instant later, the door closed again, and suddenly the house seemed very small, very close. Ellie was already huddled in the armchair, her feet drawn up beside her, hugging a faded patchwork pillow. She tried to make herself a little smaller, a little less noticeable. As if any man could fail to notice a full-grown woman in his living room.

After a time, Tommy moved farther into the room. He picked up the remote and turned off the television, then hesitated, the length of the coffee table between them.

She should say something flippant, something light, as if a few hours ago she hadn't confided her darkest secrets to him and he hadn't run screaming in the other direction.

Okay, to be fair, they were her next-to-darkest secrets, and he hadn't screamed. But he had certainly run. She'd done it enough in her lifetime to recognize it.

He shifted his weight side to side, shoved both hands into his hip pockets, then asked, "Did you tell Robbie…?"

He couldn't even say it. *That Martha was your mother, that you were a prostitute, you were in and out of jail, you were homeless, worthless, a nobody?* And she didn't say it, either. She simply nodded before asking her own question. "Did you tell Kiki?" Her bags had been in the car, and Kiki had control over the car. He must have seen her, talked to her. Repeated Ellie's secrets to her.

"Only the last part. That your name was Bethany and Martha was your mother. The rest…" He shrugged awkwardly.

Anamaria and Robbie had been sympathetic, understanding,

insisting it made no difference, though Ellie wasn't convinced. When someone told you something that shocked you, you murmured the appropriate words, but it was your behavior that told the truth. Maybe it really wouldn't change the way they felt about her; maybe they would remain her friends, or maybe they wouldn't. Only time would tell.

The truth had mattered to Tommy, and it would damn well matter to Kiki. It would give her a motive for murder once she found out the rest, which would happen sometime today, maybe tomorrow if Ellie was lucky, when they ran a criminal history on Bethany Ann Dempsey.

She'd dated a cop too long, she thought, choking back the hysterical urge to laugh. She'd picked up the terminology and knew the process undergone by suspects once they'd been arrested. If Kiki got her way, it was only a matter of time before she got to experience it firsthand instead of only in Tommy's stories.

"So now they know I have a motive, to go along with the dented car and the blood on my clothes." She swallowed hard. Robbie had been very positive and encouraging, and Anamaria couldn't have been more supportive. But Ellie wanted, needed to know the odds from someone who knew.

Her voice was smaller than she wanted it to be, and shakier, too. "Are they going to charge me?"

Tommy stiffened, and his gaze shifted away briefly before returning to her. "I'd say yes."

His answer didn't surprise her; she'd known it deep inside. She'd just hoped…and been disappointed. The reason she'd given up hoping fifteen years ago. "Did I do it? Did I run my mother down in the road?"

Finally he moved, coming to sit on the coffee table in front of her. The smell of his cologne was faint, having been applied hours ago, and a heavy growth of stubble darkened his jaw. He looked handsome, worn out and oh, so serious. "If you did, it was an accident. It was late, dark. She was wearing dark clothes. She'd been drinking. She was probably weaving down the middle of the street."

It was a picture she could envision too easily. Because she'd actually seen it? The possibility made her shudder.

"I don't believe—" He broke off abruptly, staring hard at her, then slowly, thoughtfully repeated the words. "I don't believe you did it. Accident or not. Drunk or not. I don't believe you could get so drunk that you could run over a woman in the street, get out of the car, go to her and not realize what you'd done."

"Alcoholics have blackouts all the time," she whispered, stunned that he sounded so sure when *she* didn't have a clue.

"You're not an alcoholic. If you got so drunk that you couldn't remember a damn thing all night long, would you have been able to leave the restaurant without being seen, get in your car and drive across town, run over Martha, then drive back across town and reenter the restaurant, again without being seen?"

"Do you know for sure that no one saw me leave or come back?"

"Decker told me when I picked up your stuff. They've interviewed the kitchen staff and were starting on the waiters."

Leaving unnoticed through the kitchen during business hours would be close to impossible. She always spoke to the staff when she went into the kitchen; they expected it. And they were never overly busy the night of the Halloween festival— enough to make staying open profitable, not enough to keep the staff from noticing their boss walking through their workspace.

But she could have gone out the front door. They would have assumed she was returning to the booth, so no one would have watched to see her circle the building and enter the parking lot from the alley. All the while so intoxicated that she didn't know what she was doing. And why would she have headed to the house? She'd already packed everything she wanted; she'd locked up the place and said goodbye that afternoon. There was no reason to go back

"Did they talk to Deryl, the bartender?"

"He said he served you one drink. A pumpkin-spice ale. Said you sat in the corner booth with a witch while you drank it, left right after she did, and he didn't see you again. He didn't recognize the witch's voice, but he said it was a good costume with a real heavy makeup job."

It was a scary thing, missing hours from her life, having other people know more about what she did during those hours than she did. It was even scarier having missing hours where no one knew what she'd done.

"What if I did it?" she whispered.

Tommy's mouth thinned. "You didn't."

"But what if I did? Even if no one saw me leave the restaurant, apparently I did. My car was on the other side of town. It was used to kill Martha. How would it have gotten there if I didn't drive it?"

"Someone else drove it."

She would love to believe that she'd crashed on the office sofa as soon as the ale took effect and that someone had lifted her keys and helped himself to her car. But who? People didn't just come into her office…though they could. She hadn't locked the door since the time she and Tommy had made love in there on his lunch break last spring. Someone could have walked in, found her passed out and taken her keys, then brought them back.

"Who would want to kill Martha and make it look as if I did it?"

Tommy scowled, looking fierce in spite of his fatigue. "I doubt that anyone who knew her would regret that she's dead."

That was probably true. Ellie didn't regret it, except for the fact that suspicion had been cast on her. She would say that made her a terrible daughter, but the last time she'd begged Martha to let her come home, her mother had called her a filthy whore. *You're no daughter of mine.*

Blood couldn't make up for years of neglect, bitterness and hatred.

"As for blaming you…every smart killer wants the blame to fall on somebody else. You're an easy choice. Everyone in town who saw you with Martha knew there was something ugly between you."

It was hard to be discreet when fear and disgust reeked from your very pores.

"Is there anyone Decker should be looking at?" Tommy asked. "Another relative, a friend, someone who might have come here with her, an enemy who might have followed her?"

"I've had no contact with her for almost half my life. She and my father were never close to their families. Her parents lived ten miles away, and I saw them maybe five times in fifteen years. She had a brother and two sisters, but we never saw them, either. I never even met their kids."

Silence settled between them while he scrubbed his face with his palms, then got to his feet. He disappeared into the kitchen and returned a moment later with a cold bottle of water. He offered it, she shook her head and he twisted off the cap to gulp down half of it.

"She was blackmailing you, wasn't she?"

Heat flushed Ellie, making her shift uncomfortably. "Yes. She wanted her name on the house and the business, to live with me and play the gracious hostess at the restaurant and spend my money."

"Or she would tell…" He gestured, an oddly graceful motion considering that it was filling in for words he still couldn't bring himself to say. "Did you really believe it would make a difference, Ellie? That anybody who knows you would care?"

You care, she wanted to remind him. She'd seen the shock, the revulsion. He couldn't have gotten away from her quickly enough, and he was the one who'd said he loved her.

For the first fifteen years of her life, she'd been told and shown time and again that she was nothing. Her parents had had no use for her; her best friend had helped destroy her; customers had beaten her, stolen from her and debased her; people with normal lives had kept their distance from her as if being homeless and poor and a prostitute might be contagious.

She was deeply ashamed of who she had been and what she had done. Living like that had been too painful; part of her had just wanted to curl up somewhere and die.

And part of her had struggled like hell to put those years behind her, to make herself into a new person who was, on the surface, no different than anyone else. She'd worked hard to forget that Bethany Ann Dempsey had ever existed. She'd never wanted the person she'd become tainted by even the memory of who she'd once been.

"Yes," she said flatly. "It makes a difference."

"You're wrong," he replied just as flatly. "It was a hell of a thing for you to go through, but it doesn't change anything. You're still the same woman you were yesterday. You're still the woman that people in this town know and like and respect."

She shook her head. "Only because they don't know yet. But it'll come out, and it will matter."

He stared at her a long time before grimly shaking his own head. "You don't cut people any slack, do you, Ellie? And you don't cut yourself any. You were in a bad situation, and you did what you had to to survive. If anyone holds that against you now, it's their loss, not yours."

He rubbed one hand over his face again. "I need to lie down. Promise me you won't leave."

He was asking for a promise from a woman who had lied to

him from the first time they'd met. If she said she wouldn't run away, he was willing to trust her and leave her free to do just that. The thought made a lump form in her throat. "I won't," she said, her voice hoarse.

With an accepting nod, he went to the hall, then turned back. "It'll be okay, Ellie. We'll make it so."

For the first time in days, she felt a moment of overwhelming peace. It wouldn't last long. Kiki would arrest her for Martha's death, the gossip would start and life as she knew it would end.

But for this moment, she wasn't alone. She felt safe. And even though she knew better, even though it always made the disappointment worse, for this moment she hoped.

Chapter 8

After a long, awkward evening, Tommy had been glad to get to bed. But even despite his nap that afternoon, morning came too soon. The beep of his alarm was followed a moment later by the sound of the shower coming on in the bathroom next door. He rolled onto his side and stared at the dim rectangle of light that was the window.

Of course Ellie was planning to go to work as if nothing had happened. If he'd thought about it, he would have been surprised by any other action on her part. But he hadn't thought about it.

He forced himself out of bed and went into the kitchen for a bottle of water. Though he was up at five every day but Saturdays, he wasn't a quick starter. It was sheer will that kept him moving most mornings, getting into his running clothes and shoes and setting off for the river trail and five miles to kick his brain into gear. There would be no run this morning, but no crawling back into bed, either, not unless he could persuade Ellie to go with him.

Now, there was a thought to get his blood pumping.

He'd showered and shaved the night before; by the time she came out of the bathroom, he was dressed in jeans and a T-shirt. She gave him a tight smile on her way back to Pops's room, closed the door, then came out again ten minutes later ready to leave.

"You don't have to go in," he said as he locked the front door behind them.

"This is my job. It's what I do."

"No one will think less of you if—" He broke off at the sharp look she gave him, barely visible in the thin illumination of the streetlamps.

Desperation and low self-esteem: the biggest reasons women wound up in the sex trade. Teenage girls who were thrown out by their families or who ran away because of problems at home lacked the confidence that might allow them to find some other way to survive. They were befriended by the other working girls, targeted by the pimps, easy marks because all they wanted was to stay alive and to matter to someone.

Ellie's parents deserved to burn in hell for what they'd done to her.

They drove the few minutes downtown in silence. He parked in her usual space, then followed her up the steps to the rear entrance. A lone light shone down directly overhead as she unlocked and opened the door. Then she paused. "You can go run. I'll be here."

"That's not why I'm staying," he said, and it was true. He was sticking close today in case she needed the support, in case folks proved him wrong or Kiki came by to arrest her.

With a nod, she went in, turning on lights, starting coffee.

"This place is spooky when it's empty."

She smiled for real this time. "No, it's not. It's the closest thing I've ever had to a home."

And that was just sad.

When the coffee was ready, Ellie poured two cups and stirred in sweetener, handed one to him, then left the kitchen. Instead of heading straight to her office, she stopped just outside the bar.

One light was on over the bar itself, casting deep shadows around the edges of the room. Her fingers gripped the coffee mug tightly, and her gaze was narrowed. Trying to remember Saturday night? Walking through the arched opening, talking to Deryl, sitting in one of the back booths with the woman dressed as a witch.

With a shudder, she turned away and went to her office, switched on the lights and sat down at the desk. Tommy sat in the chair nearest her. "I have no doubt Martha was devious enough to plan the blackmail scheme by herself, but was she smart enough to get proof of your background? Was she smart enough to find you?"

Ellie stared down into her coffee. "Wednesday night, the first time I saw her, she gave me copies of all my arrest reports, the photographs taken by the police, everything."

He remembered talking to her in the gazebo later that night, hearing the rustle of paper beneath her coat when she stood up. "She didn't get copies of arrest reports and booking photos of a minor legally."

"Legally or not, she had them. As for finding me, I asked her how she'd done it, and she grinned and said, 'I have my sources.'"

What kind of sources did an unemployed alcoholic woman have? "Did you change your name legally?"

"No."

"Did you keep in touch with anyone from Atlanta? Maybe someone you knew happened to come into the restaurant?"

"There was no one to stay in touch with. And if someone I knew had come here, I would have hidden in the storeroom until they left."

"Provided you saw them before they saw you."

Her nod was regretful. "When Jeffrey reserved the private dining room for Jared's birthday party, I didn't realize he would be inviting all those lawyers and judges and clients from Atlanta. I spent the whole evening in a panic that some assistant D.A. or judge would remember me."

Maybe one of them had. Maybe an old friend of Martha's had happened to pass through Copper Lake on her way someplace and recognized Ellie. Or maybe Martha had hired someone to find her. It wouldn't have been easy, but it was usually possible.

"Do you ever think about finding your mother?" Ellie asked him.

The change in subject surprised him, but he went with it. He supposed there was only so much focusing on her own troubles she could bear. "Sure. But I've never tried."

"Why not?"

"She left us. She never called, never sent a note saying 'I'm okay,' never wanted to know how we were doing without her. If I found out she was dead, that maybe she'd wound up on the streets and died all alone, I'd feel really crappy. And if I found out she'd gotten sober and made a new life for herself that didn't have room for us, I'd feel really crappy. And if she's still drinking, still miserable, still not able to cope…" He shrugged. "It's better not knowing."

She nodded a sad agreement. "Better for everyone. I never wanted anyone to know I used to be a hooker, and I bet everyone who now knows wishes they didn't. Except Kiki. She probably got a kick out of it."

"Ellie—"

Abruptly she pushed away from her desk. "I'd better see if Ramona needs any help."

Tommy hadn't heard Ramona Jackson, baker of prizewinning biscuits, breads and cheesecakes, come in, but no doubt Ellie knew her employees' routines as well as her own. Figuring she needed a break from him as well as the conversation, he let her go, settled back and drank his coffee.

By noon he'd had four cups of coffee, a full breakfast and a hefty serving of Ramona's new recipe for banana-caramel cheesecake. Ellie was hiding as much as possible from both customers and staff, and when she did have to deal with them, she was edgy and couldn't meet their gazes. When Lieutenant Decker came in a few minutes after twelve, she blanched and went stiff, then looked relieved when he beckoned Tommy out of the office.

"I got a break," Decker said once they'd reached the loading dock.

"Someone confessed to stealing Ellie's car and running down the old hag?"

"No. Isaacs's father had a heart attack while in Charlotte on business. She's gone up there with her mother." Decker raised one hand to stop Tommy from responding. "It's a minor heart attack, from what I understand, but anything that gets her out of my way is good."

Tommy couldn't help defending her, even if he shared the lieutenant's sentiments. "It's her first major case. She wants to close it quickly and make a good impression."

"I'd be more impressed if she wasn't so narrow-minded. I know she's best friends with Sophy, who has a thing for you, and you've got one for Ellie, but there's no room for bias in this business. She should have asked to be reassigned the same time you did."

"You can remove her," Tommy pointed out.

"Or I can work with her and, if not teach her something, then at least keep a tight rein on her."

Decker removed a cigarette from the pack in his shirt pocket, looked at it a moment, then put it back. Thirty hours earlier,

Tommy had stood in the same place and tried to smoke his very last cigarette. Only his shaky hands and Robbie's interference had stopped him. Today he didn't feel even the faintest desire.

After a moment, Decker gave him a sideways glance. "You know about her life as Bethany."

"Yeah."

"Poor kid."

"She thinks it'll change the way people think of her."

"It will with some of them." Decker lowered himself to sit on the edge of the dock. Tommy joined him. "I worked narcotics in Dallas for five years. A lot of my informants were prostitutes. Most people didn't think much of them, and they didn't think much of themselves. It didn't matter whether they were doing twenty-dollar blow jobs in a car or thousand-dollar-an-hour hookups in a fancy hotel, they all wanted the same thing— to get out and make a new life someplace where no one would ever know what they'd done before. And if they got that new life, their biggest fear was people finding out about the old one."

"It's no one's business what she did," Tommy said with a scowl.

"I agree. But Ellie's dreaded this for fifteen years. She's always had the fear, and you know Martha Dempsey played on it. She probably always told the kid she wasn't worth a damn, and no doubt it was easy to convince her that everyone else would think the same thing."

"I don't believe Ellie's guilty."

Decker shrugged. "The lab geeks are looking at the car and the clothes. If there's anything to find, they'll find it. Robinson's meeting me here." He glanced at his watch. "She's late."

"She's always late." Even as Tommy spoke, a county SUV pulled into the lot. Marnie Robinson climbed out, lifted a kit from the back of the vehicle, then approached them, her strides long but unhurried.

"I'm here," she said unnecessarily. Decker made a show of

looking at his watch again, but she ignored him. "Where's the bar?"

"Inside," Decker said.

"Through the kitchen and to the right," Tommy explained.

"Where's the kitchen?"

He jumped to the ground and led the way to the steps. "Haven't you ever been here?"

"I don't eat out." Her expression was dead serious when he held the door for her. "Germs."

"Wonder what else she doesn't do," Decker murmured.

The lights were on in the bar, though they didn't provide much illumination. Deryl was behind the gleaming length of mahogany, mixing up a drink that looked disgustingly like raw egg yolks. "Hey, Lieutenant. Detective." His gaze flickered over Robinson. "Lab rat."

She ignored him, too.

Decker led Markham through a recitation of Ellie's time in the bar Saturday night, having him show where the witch had sat before Ellie came in, which booth they'd occupied, which side each woman had taken.

"You clean the tables every night after closing?" Tommy asked as Robinson took out a variety of fingerprint powders.

"Yeah. And I wiped this one down as soon as they left because Ellie spilled her drink. Sorry."

Robinson continued, bypassing the tabletop for the inch-high lip that surrounded it and the bench where the witch had sat.

"She had one ale, probably twelve ounces, and spilled part of that," Decker remarked. "How much?"

"I don't know," Markham replied. "Most of it went on her clothes, but I cleaned up maybe two ounces from the table."

Tommy leaned against the bar, staring into the distance. Markham went back to his egg-yolk sludge, and Decker came to stand beside Tommy. "You thinking what I am?"

"There's no way Ellie got blackout-drunk from less than one ale."

Decker nodded. "So, unless she went someplace else when she left here and tied one on, there might be another reason for her memory loss."

"Hey, Markham," Tommy called over his shoulder. "Did Ellie pick up her drink or did you take it to her?"

"I was going to, but the witch offered because I was busy."

The perfect opportunity to dump something into the glass, give it a swirl or two, then present it to an unsuspecting victim. Guys in bars did it to girls all the time. "If she was drugged, then she couldn't have been driving the car when Martha died." Saying the words aloud sent a rush of relief through Tommy. He'd thought she was innocent—had realized it like a thump to the head when he'd sat on the coffee table the afternoon before and said, *I don't believe you did it*. Still, it was one thing for him to believe in her innocence, another entirely if the evidence supported it.

"Okay, let's go to the hospital and get her blood drawn," Decker said. "It may be too late for anything to show up, but—"

"The drug of choice for this purpose, because of its ready availability, is flunitrazepam, also known as Rohypnol," Robinson said without looking up from the prints she was collecting. "It's usually gone from the blood within six hours, but can be found in the urine for twenty-four to seventy-two hours, depending on the person's metabolic rate and how often and how much she urinates."

It had been about forty hours, so they were out of luck with the blood. They might get a hit on a urine test, though. *Might*.

"However," Robinson went on, "if she spilled the drink on her clothes, then we should find some residue on the fabric. All we've looked at is the bloodstain, which belonged to the victim, by the way. I doubt the tech even noticed the other stain."

"Let's take her over to the hospital anyway," Decker said. "Just in case."

There usually was no "just in case" with Robinson; she was always right. But Tommy was feeling pretty hopeful as he and Decker made their way to Ellie's office. The lab *would* find traces of a drug in the stain on her clothing, and she would have the satisfaction of knowing she didn't kill her mother.

So who did kill Martha Dempsey, and why were they blaming it on Ellie?

She wasn't a killer.

Though there had been no evidence of drugs in Ellie's blood, the lab had found traces of Rohypnol in her urine and in the alcohol staining the skirt and the shawl she'd worn Saturday night. Tommy's theory was straightforward: the well-dressed witch had drugged Ellie's drink, then yanked a few strands of hair from her wig, borrowed her car, run over Martha and returned the car. Unfortunately, though several of the waitresses had seen the witch, too, none had recognized her.

Ellie should have been more relieved. In truth, she just felt raw. All day long, she'd been on edge, feeling as if she must have a whole array of scarlet letters tattooed on her forehead: *M* for murderer, *P* for prostitute, *C* for criminal, *W* for worthless and whore, two of her mother's favorite words. *Had* people looked at her any differently? She couldn't say, because she'd been too ashamed to look back at them.

But everything had certainly felt different. Having a detective—even if it was Tommy—shadow her every move, A. J. Decker bringing a technician into her restaurant to treat it as if it were a crime scene, Tommy and A.J. escorting her to the emergency room to have her blood drawn... She hadn't escaped the sensation of gazes following her, judging her, until they'd returned to Tommy's house soon after the dinner rush started.

And it *was* a rush—a thirty-minute wait for a table, unusual for a Monday night. Murders were few and far between in Copper Lake; people wanted to check out the suspect in the latest. Prostitutes were few and far between there, too; maybe that was their interest in her. Maybe they'd thought her own restaurant was the best place to hear the latest gossip, or they wanted to supplement their own gossip. *Why, I saw her last night, and she looked like she couldn't care less about all the fuss.* Or *She looked pretty ragged, so it must be true. A thief and a whore in our midst! How did we not see it sooner?*

Go home, Carmen had advised, and after a long day, Ellie had been happy to obey. After all, she wasn't of any use to the staff when she was afraid to leave her office. Now she sat at the table that filled Tommy's small dining room, the remains of dinner in front of her. Anamaria and Robbie had come over, bringing the food with them, a spicy recipe passed down through generations of Anamaria's family from one of her Cuban or Haitian ancestors. Ellie had eaten her share but remembered nothing else about it.

"Let's let the men do dishes," Anamaria said, bumping against Ellie's shoulder to get her attention. "We'll take our tea out on the deck and enjoy knowing that they're doing the work."

Gratefully Ellie followed her out. All Tommy and Robbie had talked about was the case, until she thought her head might explode. She was so sick of thinking, talking, wondering, worrying. She just wanted…

She wanted life to go back to the way it was before Martha had shown up in town. No, to the way it was a year ago, when Tommy was still satisfied with what she could give him. She'd loved having him in her life, loved the sex and the companionship and loving him and being loved by him.

Loving him. She'd never told him. She'd always been fearful of her past, of being hurt, betrayed, abandoned, outed. If she never acknowledged, even to herself, that she loved him, then somehow she would be safer. He could break up with her, which he had, but as long as she'd never said *I love you,* her heart wouldn't break.

Her logic had been a bit faulty.

The evening was cool, the tea hot in sturdy porcelain mugs. They sat side by side on the steps, Anamaria easing herself down with a laugh. "Mama Odette says I'm gonna be big as a house before this girl comes. Sometimes I wonder if there's a second one in there, hiding behind the first."

"You're a lucky woman," Ellie said quietly.

"So are you."

She resisted declaring her disagreement with a vehement snort. She had been lucky for five years. But luck couldn't last forever, neither good nor bad. *This, too, shall pass.*

But what would she have left when it was over?

Anamaria gave her a sidelong look. "Have I ever told you about my mother?" She briefly paused for Ellie's *No.* "Her name was Glory, and she was a beautiful woman. She was also a kept woman. At least, that's what some people called her. Easy, slut, whore…different people, different names. But that was how she supported herself and me. She always had a handful of regular clients, and she saw them once or twice or five times a month. She satisfied them sexually, and they satisfied her financially."

Ellie had known most of the girls working her territory fifteen years ago, had been friends with some and disliked others. But she'd never known anyone who'd escaped the streets and made it into the world of escort or mistress. It was safer sex, more money, less humiliating, but it was still prostitution. "Why did she do it?"

"She liked men, she liked sex and she liked money. Much more frivolous reasons than yours." Anamaria's shrug was a blur in Ellie's peripheral vision. "She had choices. She was smart and clever and a good psychic. She turned down more marriage proposals than most women ever get. She had no need of a husband. She wanted to live life on her terms, and if anyone disapproved, she laughed in their faces."

"And yet you got married."

"I'm living life on *my* terms." Anamaria's sweet smile faded as she laid her hand on Ellie's arm. "Mama chose that life for herself, and she accepted the consequences that came with it. You didn't have a choice, Ellie. You didn't run away from home, you didn't want to live on the streets, you didn't want to have sex with strangers. You've already paid dearly for the misfortune of having bad parents. You can't keep punishing yourself for it."

Ellie stared off into the shadows, blinking to clear her eyes. "Before everything fell apart, I was looking at colleges and scholarships and grants. I wanted to be a doctor or a teacher. I planned to get established in my career, then fall in love and get married and have children. I was going to live in a small town, in a house with a picket fence, with bicycles in the front yard and a puppy in the back. I wanted the kind of family and home I'd never had, and I really believed I could have it, if I just worked hard enough.

"Then, in less than twenty-four hours, I lost every dream I'd ever had. My future shrank from all these huge possibilities down to one—staying alive for another day." She glanced at Anamaria, getting an impression of sympathy, but she couldn't hold the look for more than a second. "I had always been such a good girl with this huge fear of retribution. I never broke the rules, disrespected a teacher, told a lie or cheated on an assignment. The kids called me Goody Two-shoes. Afterward, every time I got arrested, every time I broke another law, even if it was the difference between surviving or not, I was so ashamed."

"That was because you had a conscience," Anamaria said quietly. "You knew the difference between right and wrong, and you cared. If you were a bad person, Ellie, you wouldn't have been ashamed, you wouldn't have feared retribution and you wouldn't have lived an honest, moral life ever since."

"But I did so much awful stuff," Ellie whispered. And not just on the street. She'd committed her biggest sin after getting off the streets, after months of living in a trendy condo, wearing the nicest clothes she'd ever owned and eating at Atlanta's best restaurants.

"You had two choices, Ellie—fight for yourself by doing what was necessary to survive, or give up and become just one more kid who died tragically young." Anamaria moved close enough to slide her arm around Ellie's shoulders. "Let me tell you, giving up would have been a tragic loss for all of us who love you."

Ellie resisted a moment, the old habit of trying to hold back, then sank into Anamaria's embrace. Her friend smelled of tropical flowers and cocoa butter, and a wealth of positive emotion radiated from her, warming Ellie, taking the sharp edge off her own feelings.

Baby Gloriane was never going to lack for love and protection and a safe place in her mother's arms. Martha had never offered any of that to Ellie, and at eighteen, Ellie had known nothing she could offer her own little girl would be enough. She was too broken. Too damaged.

The back door opened with a creak, and Ellie quickly swiped her hand across her eyes. It was Robbie, though, and he didn't step out. "Annie, we need to go, babe."

Anamaria's arm tightened for a moment around Ellie; then she let go and, with one hand on the railing, pulled herself to her feet. She paused a moment, her hand stretched out to but not touching Ellie. "You'll come through this, intact, stronger than ever and happy. Really happy."

Ellie's smile was unsteady. "Is that a vision or wishful thinking?"

"The great-great-granddaughter of Queen Moon does not engage in wishful thinking," she intoned before lightening up. "Take it as you will. Just know that I'll say 'I told you so' when it comes true."

"I'll be happy to hear it." *If* it came true.

Ellie said goodbye to Robbie, then directed her gaze out into the night again. It was a bit too chilly for comfort now that Anamaria was gone, but it was quiet. Peaceful. She desperately needed quiet and peace.

The sound of car doors closing echoed loudly in the darkness. A moment later, the back door opened again, footsteps moving across the deck. Something warm brushed her as Tommy wrapped the afghan from the sofa around her shoulders before sitting next to her.

The yarn was soft, fuzzy and smelled comfortingly of his cologne. She buried her face in it, breathing deeply of the fragrance that had once been such a part of her life. It had made her feel warm, desired, happy, loved, aroused.

Happy.

Aware of him sitting so close but, like her, gazing into the dark, Ellie straightened her shoulders, grasping the ends of the afghan like a shawl. "The great-great-granddaughter of Queen Moon says I'm going to come out of this mess a happy woman."

He glanced at her, his expression unreadable. "I tend to believe what Anamaria says." Then, after a time… "What do you say?"

She tried for a light note, because there was absolutely nothing light about the way she was feeling. "She's terribly optimistic."

"That's just another way of saying hopeful, and that's not a bad thing, Ellie. You could use a little hope yourself."

"I hoped for a long time, Tommy. I hoped I would get a scholarship so I could go to college. I hoped I would move out of my parents' house and never see them again. When they threw me out, I hoped they would let me come back, because I didn't have what it took to be on my own. I hoped I didn't get caught stealing. When I was running errands for drug dealers, I hoped I didn't get caught in a drive-by shooting or a drug bust. I hoped I'd never have to sell my body, and I hoped and prayed the second time wouldn't be even a fraction as painful and horrible as the first. I kept hoping and hoping until I finally learned—if you never hope for anything, you won't be disappointed."

"That's tough on your spirit," he murmured.

"Not as tough as always being disappointed." That had broken her spirit: the realization that she couldn't have a normal life. For whatever reason, God or the Fates had decided she didn't deserve it. How could she have hope for anything after learning that?

Tommy's hand went to his shirt pocket, looking for a cigarette that wasn't there, she surmised, smiling humorlessly. What was it about her that made people want to slowly poison themselves? Her father, her mother, Tommy…

He shifted on the steps to face her, the newel post at his back. "I know our parents and our childhoods have a huge impact on who we become and what we do and how we feel about ourselves. I know your parents put you through hell, and I understand what that did to you inside. But at the same time, I just want to say get over it. You're a beautiful, intelligent, successful woman. You have your own house, your own business, friends and people who respect you. Even if you'd really had the fantasy upbringing that you claimed, you'd be a success by anyone's standards. But considering your real background, it's nothing less than amazing.

"You've got so much to be proud of, Ellie. You not only survived, but you thrived. Whether in spite of your past or because of it, you've done damn good. Robbie and Anamaria and I—we're proud of you. Why can't you be?"

There were few moments in life that she remembered with pride. No one else had ever been proud of her; why should she be impressed with her own accomplishments? She'd done nothing special. She *was* nothing special.

Except, maybe, in Tommy's eyes.

The thought brought tears to her own eyes. "Really?" she questioned, forcing cynicism into her voice because his words gave rise to a bit of hope deep inside her, and, as she'd just told him, never hoping was better than being disappointed. "Which me are you proud of? The kid whose parents couldn't love her? The girl with the arrest record a mile long? The teenage prostitute? The one who created a false identity? The one who lied to you about everything? The one who kept pushing you away because she had nothing to give? Which me are you so damn proud of?"

He reached out then and touched her, his fingers warm against her cheek, his touch light and gentle and so familiar, God help her, that she wanted to curl into it. "You can't separate them, Ellie. They're all you. They all combine to make you the woman you are now. How could I love one of them without loving all of them?"

She stared at him. The smart thing to do was ignore his words. Get up, walk into the house and shut herself away in her bedroom. Pretend the words had never been spoken. She summoned the strength to do just that, but instead of rising from the steps, she raised one hand to clasp his wrist. Instead of walking away, she asked, "You can still say that?"

He smiled ruefully. "Only because it's true. Hell, Ellie, I've loved you practically since the day we met."

"But you never really knew me."

"I've always known the things that matter. All this stuff…it's just background. I'm glad I know, but it doesn't change anything."

Her stomach knotted, and something fluttered in her chest, panic trying to find a way out, as she forced a breath.

"Well…before you swear to that, let me tell you the last bit of background, because it might change everything. Let me tell you about the baby girl I gave away for fifty thousand dollars."

There was this guy…

A lot of hard-luck stories started out that way, and Tommy had heard his share. Sometimes he'd empathized; sometimes he'd wondered how women could be so easily fooled; but never had he dreaded the details as much as he did now. If Ellie had kept this secret after confiding everything else, it must be seriously important to her, and that made it just as important to him. She'd expected him to turn away from her after hearing the truth about her criminal history, but he hadn't. Apparently, she thought this truth might accomplish what the other hadn't.

"I was seventeen, still on the streets, and I'd met my quota for the night. It was cold, so I went to this all-night diner to get a cup of coffee." Unlike before, when she'd hardly been able to look at him, she kept her gaze locked on him, searching for the slightest change in expression. It was an effort, but he kept his face blank and his posture relaxed while he listened.

"His name was Andrew. He'd been out partying and stopped there on his way home for some food. He so obviously didn't belong in that part of town. His clothes, his watch, his car…there were dollar signs practically dancing in the air around him. He sat at the table next to mine and struck up a conversation, and we talked for more than two hours."

It was easy to imagine: a vulnerable girl whose only value to anyone was sex and a rich man interested in her, not her body. He'd probably bought her coffee, flirted with her and made her feel like any teenage girl on a date with her biggest crush.

"He asked me to come back the next night and the night after that. The fourth night, I went home with him. He was the first man I—" Her mouth flattened, and she swallowed hard. "The first man I wanted to have sex with. To—to make love with. He was everything I'd dreamed of before…" Her shrug said what she didn't: before she lost her virginity to a john who'd made her pray that the next time wouldn't hurt so bad.

"I wanted so much to be saved, and he wanted to do it. He rented a condo for me, bought me fabulous clothes and gave me more money than I'd ever seen. He said he loved me and he wanted to marry me." Her smile was thin and painful. "This rich, gorgeous guy wanted to marry *me*. It was incredible. Like Julia Roberts in *Pretty Woman*."

Except *Pretty Woman* was a fairy tale. *And they lived happily ever after*. Ellie's Prince Charming had turned into a toad.

"I was so much in love and so blissfully unaware. When I got pregnant, I thought life couldn't be any more perfect. I told him, and…" Even after so many years, there was a faint undercurrent of hurt in her voice. "He walked out on me."

Tommy let his gaze drop to her hands, wrapped tightly in the fringe of the afghan. He didn't want to hear any more; it was all in the past; it didn't matter.

But of course it did. To her. To him.

"He quit paying the rent on the condo, so I had to move out. I'd saved some of the money he'd given me, and I sold everything he'd bought for me, so I managed to get by for a while. I was seven months pregnant when the money ran out. I didn't know what to do. I tried to get in touch with him, but he wouldn't return my calls. Finally, I threatened to show up at his family home in Athens. The next day, his uncle, who was also his attorney, contacted me.

"Part of his uncle's job was cleaning up Andrew's messes," she went on, her tone cool and detached. "You see, he was already married to a woman from a family as influential as his own. And I wasn't the first underage girl he'd gotten pregnant. In fact, Uncle Randolph had the routine down pat. He moved me into an apartment in Alpharetta. He paid my living expenses. He promised to find a really good home for the baby, and he gave me fifty thousand dollars in exchange for forgetting that Andrew existed."

She'd been in love with another man. She'd given birth to another man's child. And for four and a half years, she'd refused to even consider marrying Tommy. Because she hadn't loved him? Because she couldn't love him?

Or because the first bastard had hurt her too damn much to risk it again?

If you never hope for anything, you won't be disappointed.

The biggest part of her life had been nothing but one disappointment after another.

"I had a girl." Ellie's voice was hollow, insubstantial in the night. "She was seventeen inches long and she weighed eight pounds, and I held her for a minute. I kissed her and told her I loved her and I was giving her up for her own good. Then I handed her back to the nurse, and…I died a little inside."

Her last words were barely a whisper; then she fell silent, waiting for him to say something.

For five years he'd wanted intimacy with her. To know everything about her. To become a part of her. To make her a part of himself. Who knew intimacy could hurt as much as the lack of it?

His voice was ragged when he finally spoke. "Is that it? No more secrets?"

She stared at him.

"Because I can take just about anything, Ellie, but it's kind of hard taking it all at once."

One slender hand slid out from under the shawl, and she wrapped her fingers tightly around his. "Did you listen to what I said, Tommy? I gave up my baby girl. I traded her and the promise of secrecy for money. I abandoned her, just like your mother left you."

He twisted his hand so he held hers. "You were a child who gave your own child a chance at a better life. My mother was older than you are now, and she walked away from her family because it suited her. It's not the same, and you know it. You loved your baby enough to leave. My mother didn't love me enough to stay."

She tried to push away, so he caught both her hands in his. "I couldn't take care of her," she said, her voice thick with tears. "I couldn't even take care of myself."

"But you did take care of her, Ellie. You gave her to someone who would love her and protect her and give her all the things you never had." She'd broken her own heart, and just listening to her talk about it damn near broke his.

The tension holding her stiff eased a bit.

"I wish like hell things had been different for you. I wish you'd never had to go through all that crap. I wish you'd had a boringly normal life with no worries more important than whether the boy you liked was going to ask you to the prom. But like I keep telling you, it doesn't matter. I'm sorry, and I'd really like to break this Andrew guy in half. But it's in the past. It doesn't matter."

The look in her eyes was faint and alien, for her at least. He saw it in his own eyes every time he looked in the mirror. "It doesn't bother you that I was in love with him?" she asked with the slightest undertone of hope.

He brushed a strand of her pale blond hair back before grinning crookedly. "You were twenty-five when we met. I never expected to be the first guy you loved. I just hoped to be the last."

For a moment she showed no response. She just looked at him, her expression puzzled, as if she wanted to believe what he was saying but couldn't quite. Then, with a shudder, she pulled the afghan closer, huddling into it, looking lost and vulnerable and confused. "I—I—"

Jumping to her feet, she rushed across the deck and inside the house, closing the back door hard but not before he heard the small choke of a half-swallowed sob.

Eyes closed, head falling back, Tommy breathed loudly. As he'd told her, he could take just about anything. But it damn sure wasn't easy.

Not that Ellie had ever been easy, he thought with a thin smile. But she was worth it. The two of them *together*—if they could work out a together—was worth all the heartache in the world.

Chapter 9

After a restless night, Ellie was up early Tuesday morning. She looked worn-out when she studied herself in the mirror; makeup couldn't hide the shadows beneath her eyes or the lines at the corners of her mouth. But there was something different in her face this morning: doubt.

She'd told Tommy everything, and he'd said it didn't matter. Her worst memories and most painful secrets, her flaws and insecurities and her ugly past, and to him it was just background. It didn't change the way he looked at her. Didn't change the way he thought of her. He still found her worthy.

How incredible was that?

Maybe he was right—Anamaria and Robbie, too. Maybe her parents had lied to her all those years and she did deserve love and respect and friendship and a normal life.

Maybe she was a better person than she'd given herself credit for.

Tommy slept in, probably the first weekday morning in his adult life, and, unsettled inside, she let him. She fixed a cup of coffee, found a protein bar in the cabinet—the only thing in the kitchen that even came close to breakfast food—then wrapped the afghan around her shoulders and went outside to sit in a rocker on the front porch.

The morning was still, the streetlamps buzzing, a few house-lights on here and there. Occasionally a car passed at the end of the block, or a boat on the nearby river, but mostly it was quiet. Chilly. Soothing.

She'd finished with breakfast but was still rocking slowly, the empty coffee mug cradled in her hands, when a dark vehicle turned onto the street. The headlights flashed across her as the driver pulled into the driveway; an instant later, the engine cut off. A. J. Decker climbed out, pushing the door shut with a con-trolled thud, then joined her on the porch, leaning against the railing in front of her.

He looked as if he'd had a restless night, too. Short as his hair was, it stood on end, and he wore a layer of weariness as easily as his leather jacket.

"Where's Maricci?" As if in deference to the quiet morning, A.J.'s words were pitched low. His voice was gravelly, as if it, too, needed rest.

"Not up yet when I came out."

"So this is how he keeps an eye on a flight risk."

She smiled faintly. "I'm not a flight risk. Not anymore."

"Since you slipped a little in your position as our primary suspect?"

"Since the truth began coming out." Actually, since Sunday afternoon, when Tommy asked for her promise that she wouldn't leave. When he'd shown his willingness to trust her.

"'And the truth shall set you free.'" There was a hint of cynicism to his voice.

Again she smiled. "I associated a lot of things with telling the truth—horror, fear, revulsion, disappointment—but not freedom. But it is freeing in a way. The thing I feared most has happened. People know the worst. What they do with it…"

"Is out of your control. Anyone who has a problem with it isn't worth having around anyway." He rubbed one hand across his face. "I got a report from the lab on your car."

"Good news or bad?" The voice came from behind Ellie an instant before the screen door creaked open and Tommy came out. He wore jeans and a Clemson T-shirt, faded and snug, and his feet were bare. If he realized it was too chilly for bare feet and arms, he didn't show it.

A.J. acknowledged him by directing his reply to Tommy. "It was definitely the car used to run down Martha Dempsey. The blood on the hood, the flecks of paint on her body, the fibers caught in the dent—all match. But there aren't any fingerprints. Not on the steering wheel, the gearshift or the door handle."

Tommy grunted as he lifted himself onto a section of porch railing.

Ellie looked from one man to the other. "Did you expect to find fingerprints?"

"We expected to find yours," A.J. answered. "You do drive the car every day."

"It suggests that you weren't the last person to drive it, that whoever was wiped it clean," Tommy added.

"Or that you wiped the prints in the hopes that we would assume someone else had done it."

Maybe it was the early hour, or maybe her mind just wasn't devious enough, but it took her a moment to understand what they meant. If she'd been the one to kill Martha, there would have been no need to get rid of the fingerprints; hers were supposed to be there. The only logical reason to clean them away was if they didn't belong. Or to build an alibi.

"And then what? I went back to the restaurant and drugged myself to make myself look innocent?" She'd meant to be flippant, but it came out laced with panic instead. The coffee cup shifted as her fingers went numb. Drawing a breath, she carefully set it on the floor, then clasped her hands together. She'd taken such relief in finding out that her drink had been drugged; she'd seen it as proof that she hadn't been involved in Martha's death.

But in truth, her involvement was still a possibility. Those nine hours were still missing. She had no clue what she'd done.

Her mouth didn't want to open, her voice to form the words, but she forced them. "Oh God. You're saying I might have killed my mother and tried to throw off the police."

"No." Both men answered at once, Tommy's tone more emphatic than A.J.'s.

"We know what time you had the drink," A.J. explained, "and we know what time the victim died. By then, you would have needed help keeping your eyes open. There's no way you could have been driving that car."

Unless the drug was another part of her plan. What if there'd been nothing in her ale at the bar but ale, if she'd mixed the drug in later and poured it on her clothes to make it appear as a spill? What if she really had slipped out of the restaurant, killed Martha, wiped the car clean, drugged herself—

Suddenly Tommy's foot landed on the arm of the chair, stopping her agitated rocking, and he scowled at her. "Stop it. You didn't come up with some elaborate scheme to kill your mother. This was premeditated. Whoever killed Martha planned to do it, and planned to frame you. She had the drug ready. She made sure you were out of the way, and then she hung back and watched Martha until she had her chance." His look was supremely annoyed. "You don't even know how to get hold of Rohypnol."

He was right. In her time on the streets, she could have

gotten anything. But that was a long time ago. She didn't have a clue where to look today. Didn't want a clue.

He took her silence as agreement. "Your memory loss affects only the hours after you were drugged. Everything before then and since is clear. If you'd planned to murder Martha, you would remember it."

There wasn't a blank time in her entire life except for those hours. She could recite every detail of Saturday evening, right up to the time she'd talked to Deryl at the bar. *What's hot?*

Tommy was right. She would remember.

"In other news," A.J. said, drawing her attention back to him, "I asked a cop friend in Atlanta to go by the victim's house yesterday and talk to her neighbors. The house had been broken into and ransacked. No one saw or heard anything, and there's no way to tell if anything's missing. It could have been some lowlife who plans his burglaries with the obituaries, or it could have been the killer."

Retrieving anything that might connect the killer to Martha.

Huddled inside the afghan, breathing steadily of Tommy's scent, Ellie tried to force even the faintest of memories of the witch she'd drunk with in the bar. For God's sake, she'd sat across from the woman, chatting with her, and the whole time, the woman had been biding her time until she could kill Ellie's mother.

And thanks to the drug, Ellie couldn't remember a thing.

The woman must have been a coldhearted snake. Of course, that was an apt description of Martha, too. Like gravitated to like.

"Did they find anything having to do with me at Martha's house?" she asked hesitantly.

A.J. looked away a moment, as if he'd rather not answer, then shook his head. "Nothing."

No copies of her arrest reports or booking photos. No

school pictures of her, no baby pictures. No reminders of the daughter Martha had abandoned until, suddenly, she'd found a new use for her.

It didn't hurt as much as she might have expected.

"When I first saw her, she had copies of my arrest record."

"We didn't find them. Not at her house, not on her and not at the bed-and-breakfast," A.J. said. "I'm guessing the killer gave them to her and also took them away."

"Who would have access to that information?"

"The police," Tommy answered. "The court. The public defender's office."

She smiled thinly. She'd had a different lawyer for each arrest, usually young, earnest people who'd still believed they could make a difference in their clients' lives. *Don't get attached,* one of the other girls had told her. *They don't last long.*

Nobody in Ellie's experience had lasted long.

Then she glanced at Tommy and amended that. He'd stuck with her long after any reasonable man would have walked away. Four and a half years, ups and downs, good and bad, he'd been there. And when things had gotten really bad, he'd come back. He'd believed in her, helped her to believe in herself.

"Jared and Jeffrey didn't see anyone at the bed-and-breakfast?" she asked.

"Martha's room had a private entrance," A.J. replied. "As far as they know, she didn't have any visitors. The last time they saw her was around seven Saturday evening."

Tommy slid to his feet, then leaned against the rail. "If her killer was also her accomplice, she must have taken Martha's key, cleaned out her room, then returned the key before her body was discovered."

A coldhearted snake. Ellie huddled deeper into the afghan. "Now what?"

A.J. shrugged. "We keep asking questions. Looking for

answers. Try to find someone else with as much reason to want the victim dead as you had."

Her stomach knotting, Ellie abruptly rose and went inside the house, leaving the door open and the two men talking quietly behind her. She didn't slow until she was in the darkened kitchen, muscles clenched, nausea swirling inside her, standing at the sink, staring out the window at nothing.

She wasn't off the prime suspect list yet. Right now an argument could be made for her guilt as easily as her innocence. Lack of fingerprints on the car? The killer wiped it clean, or she did. The drugs in her system? Slipped by the killer into her drink, or taken deliberately on her own after the murder. Motive? Martha's blackmail accomplice had wanted to silence her, or a bitter, angry daughter had wanted to end the blackmail.

Without Martha's copies of the arrest records, Ellie couldn't even prove there'd been a blackmail attempt. As far as Tommy and A.J. knew, she could have made that up to provide another suspect for the killing.

As far as *she* knew, she could be guilty.

The screen door closed, then the front door. A moment later bare feet sounded on the floor, muffled on ancient rugs, sharper on wood. The steps came straight to her, and before she could react, before she could even stiffen, Tommy wrapped his arms around her from behind.

She didn't think about pushing him away, as she'd been doing for far too long. She leaned back against him, immediately feeling the heat of his body through the afghan, and lifted her hands to clasp his. "I hate this."

"I know."

"I could be guilty."

"No, you couldn't."

"Those nine hours I lost…"

"They were taken from you," he corrected. "By the killer."

"I want them back."

His breath rustled her hair. "That's probably not going to happen, babe."

The doctor had told her that at the hospital the day before. It wasn't fair. Things she would dearly love to forget remained crystal clear in her mind after fifteen years, and events she desperately needed to remember would likely remain a blank forever.

Tommy sighed again. "Decker said the medical examiner is releasing Martha's body today. What do you want to do?"

Do? What was there to—

A funeral. Burial. That was what daughters normally did when their mothers died. She'd never imagined picking out a casket for Martha, had never imagined even knowing when either of her parents died. "I suppose she should be buried next to my father." Her voice took on a thick, clogged quality. "I don't even know where that is."

"I'll find out." His mouth nuzzled closer to her ear. "It's okay to cry, Ellie. She may have been lousy at it, but she was still your mother."

She opened her mouth to insist that she had no tears to shed over the mother she'd never had, but a sob came out instead. She turned in his arms until they were facing, her cheek pressing against his shirt, and she wept angry, bitter, heartsore tears. A lousy mother, a lousy father, a lousy family. Her only remaining relatives were total strangers, sharing nothing with her but genetics. She was thirty and alone in a way she'd never been.

Though she'd been alone in all the ways that mattered for half her life, she deserved better than that. She didn't mourn Martha's death. She was just mourning what should have been.

When the tears slowed, she raised her head to look at Tommy in the lightening room. "A.J.'s wrong. I didn't want her dead. Just out of my life."

"He knows that. He's just thinking like a cop."

She swiped one hand across her cheeks to dry them. "And what are you thinking like?"

Tommy stared at her a long, still moment, his face mere inches away, his dark gaze steady and intense. Something passed through it—hesitation, doubt—then he quietly answered, "A man who loves you."

She'd heard the words from him before and had treasured them every time, but she'd known they were always based on fantasy: the woman he thought she was, the normal, average, undamaged woman she'd pretended to be. But now he knew that woman had never existed, and he could still talk about her and love in the same breath. He could still sound as if he meant it.

Her hand trembled when she lifted it to his face, when she grazed her fingers across his cheek. He'd showered and shaved while she was out on the porch; he smelled of soap and shampoo, and his jaw was smooth as silk. He was unbearably handsome, and serious, and good, and he loved her. *Her.* What did it matter if her mother and father hadn't? What did anyone matter besides him?

Ellie rose onto her toes, her lips following the same trail her fingers had taken, touching his cheek here, brushing his jaw there, stroking her tongue across that sensitive spot at the corner of his mouth. He remained motionless a moment, and for one panicked instant, she wondered if loving her despite the fact that she'd been a prostitute and making love to her knowing she'd been a prostitute were two different matters for him.

Then he turned his head the few inches necessary to claim her mouth, and he pulled her closer, hard against his body, against his arousal, and the panic faded.

So long... Since he'd held her, since he'd kissed her, since she'd felt safe in his arms. So long since she'd felt his warmth and savored just the pure sweetness of him, and always before, no matter how right it seemed, she'd felt unworthy. This morning she felt as if she'd come home.

She didn't know if she initiated the kiss or he did, but suddenly his lips were on hers, his tongue probing, his mouth stealing the very breath from her. She clung to him, lost herself in him, protesting with a soft whimper when he broke away and pulled back far enough to gaze down at her.

"The first time I saw you…" His voice was hoarse, unsteady, his breathing ragged. "Someone had reported an intruder at the old general store. The front door was locked, so I went around to the back. When I went in, you were standing where the bar is now, turning around slowly with your arms open wide and this look on your face, and I thought, 'Damn, she's beautiful.'" He touched one hand gently to her cheek. "And, 'Damn, she's hot.'" His fingers brushed across her jaw to her throat. "And, 'Damn, I want her.'" Warm and callused, they skimmed the neckline of her shirt and made her skin ripple. "That's never changed, Ellie. It never will."

Never. What an incredibly lovely word, ranking right up there with *love* and *always,* the kind a woman could wrap around herself and delight in.

To keep the tears at bay, she asked, "What look?"

He loosened the top button of her shirt, then the second, touching her more than was necessary, less than she needed. "Happiness. You were totally, unquestionably happy."

She remembered the day, of course. She'd just signed the papers on the building, taking on a debt that, ten years earlier, would have seemed impossible. To save money, she was going to live in the cramped rooms above the restaurant, now an elegant private dining room, and she was committing to a future of long days and hard work. But she'd allowed herself that one moment of pure bliss. She'd had a dream and the chance to make it come true. More than she'd had for so many years.

With her top unbuttoned, his hands were at her waist now, and he was slowly backing her against the counter as his mouth teased back and forth along her jaw. An intense desire to surrender completely to the sensation—to stop talking, stop thinking—made her voice thin when she pushed ahead.

"I looked at you and thought, 'God, he's gorgeous.' And then you showed me your badge, and I just wanted to run away and hide."

"I never knew. Not then. Not the first time we kissed. Not the first time you tempted me upstairs and into your bed."

Her laugh startled her. "You talk as if some time actually passed between all that. And I think you were the one doing the tempting."

"Twenty-six hours. And you definitely were the seducer. All I did was kiss you—" he did it again "—and touch you here—" he brushed her throat again "—and here—"

The thin silk and lace of her bra provided no barrier to his caress. She felt every degree of heat in his palm and every scrape of his rough skin. Her nipple swelled before he reached it, the ache intensifying when he ducked his head to kiss it.

"And you suggested we go upstairs to your bedroom. It was your idea." His grin was smug, sexy, at odds with the fierce hunger in his eyes.

"Because I didn't want to have sex in the kitchen," she weakly protested.

"And here we are in the kitchen again. Do you still prefer beds over countertops?"

"I do."

His breath feathered over her ear, making her shiver. "Lucky me. I have one just a few yards away." Taking her hand, he led her out of the kitchen, a quick turn through the hall, into his bedroom and straight to the bed.

His kiss was leisurely, lazy, as if he knew they had the rest of their lives to enjoy it. He nuzzled her mouth, wet her lips with his tongue, then nipped her lower lip before sliding his tongue inside.

Lifting hands that trembled, she skimmed her palms across his cheeks, then down to his chest, broad and muscular, tapering to a narrow waist and narrower hips. The cotton of his shirt was soft and fitted snugly. She curled her fingers in it and tugged it free of his jeans. When she slid her hands underneath to the heated silk of his skin, over rock-hard muscles and flat nipples, then swept back down to the button of his jeans, he made a guttural sound and his tongue stabbed deeper. When she managed, with much fumbling, to undo the button and zipper, his groan vibrated through her.

He caught her wrist, pulled her hand away from his arousal and undid her own button and zipper. They broke apart long enough to shuck the rest of their clothes and find a condom in the nightstand drawer, then tumbled onto the bed in a tangle of limbs.

He pushed into her, quick, hard, deep, no longer interested in taking his time. She savored the connection for a moment, the familiar warmth, then arched her hips, rubbing tantalizingly against his length, drawing another groan from him.

With one hand on either side of her head, he braced himself above her, staring down at her, his gaze dark. "God, I've missed you."

Once more tears stung her eyes. She'd cried during sex before, but never good tears. She'd wept every one of the first dozen times, until something inside her had died and she'd just gone numb in its place.

Nothing was numb now. Her nerves tingled, her muscles contracted, her nipples hardened. Heat flowed with her blood, and her heartbeat competed with the ragged rasp of her breathing to echo in her ears. She felt alive. Desired.

Loved.

"I've missed you, too," she whispered. "I never meant to hurt you."

He lowered himself until his forehead rested, warm and damp, against hers. "I know."

"I was just…" Her throat clogged, and she dashed away a tear before touching his face. He turned to press a kiss to her palm.

"Afraid," he finished for her. "I understand. But from now on, when you're afraid, you come to me. Don't push me away. Let me be strong when you need it, and you be strong when I do."

Her smile was teary, her lungs tight, and though she tried to tease, there was a hiccup in her voice. "When have you ever needed someone else's strength?"

"Every day of my life, darlin'. Especially—" his breath hitched, and his voice turned dark and strained "—right now. I can't… Damn it, not yet …"

She knew just how to make him finish quickly—how to move against him, how to clench muscles deep inside around him, how to make his body stiffen and his breath stop and his vision go dark.

And he knew exactly how to do the same to her. Her gasp was soundless, heat flaring through her like wildfire, everything quivering and trembling as sensation grew wickedly sharp, clawing, then exploding. She clung to him, eyes squeezed shut, body damn near humming, and he held her through his own orgasm, offering thick guttural words that were little more than a soothing whisper underlying the pounding of her heart.

God, I've missed you, he'd said, and tears seeped from her eyes as she pressed her face to his shoulder.

She'd been worth missing.

Imagine that.

Instead of growing lighter outside, sometime in the last half hour, it had gotten darker, and now thunder rumbled somewhere far off. In Tommy's opinion, it was a good morning for staying in bed. Sleep an hour or two, make love again, listen to the rain…

Ellie was so still that he might have thought she was asleep if he hadn't known better. Good sex made some women drowsy, but it always left her wanting to talk. It was nice knowing that about her.

It was better knowing everything else.

"Thank you."

He lay on his side, snuggled skin to skin with her, her soft murmur vibrating through him. His right arm was over her waist, and her silky blond hair was just a breath from his mouth, too tempting to ignore, so he didn't. Nuzzling it aside, breathing in the fresh citrusy scent of her shampoo, he brought his mouth near her ear. "You're welcome."

He didn't ask what she was thanking him for. He could think of a dozen answers she might give, and specifics didn't really matter. And she was welcome. In so many more ways than the trite phrase implied.

The rain started then, and she breathed deeply as if she could smell it through the closed windows. They'd made love in the rain once. On the beach. In the middle of the day. It had been a slow week at the deli, so they'd taken off for a few days at one of South Carolina's barrier islands. It had been an experience—torrential rain, surf pounding, no one in their little corner of the world but them.

Sex in an unusual place had been more a novelty for him than her, he now knew. But she'd had a choice with him. She'd chosen to get involved with him, to be with him.

To not marry him.

"Ellie."

"Hmm."

"I still want to get married."

She froze, but she didn't try to pull away or change the

subject. Instead, she wriggled around until she was facing him, in the process giving him the beginnings of another hard-on. Her expression wasn't the cool blank he'd grown accustomed to whenever the subject came up. It was pretty damn wary. "Do you still want to marry me?"

He collapsed on his back with a great dramatic grunt. "God, you're killing me. Of course I want to marry you. Would I be here now if I was planning to propose to someone else?"

She didn't answer but raised herself onto one elbow to see him better.

"I've been telling you for about four years that I love you. I want to marry you. I want to grow old with you." He hesitated, then went for broke. "I want to have kids with you, El. I want it all." He stared at her, searching for some response. Her muscles didn't tense. Her breath didn't catch or her eyes fill with tears. She didn't jump out of bed and start searching for her clothes. She just stared back at him.

His hand shook as he stroked her cheek. "The kids aren't a deal-breaker. If you can't face that…it's okay."

They might have been the hardest words he'd ever said— well, second to the ultimatum he'd given her six months ago. He'd always been close to his father and to Pops; whenever he'd imagined himself grown up and married, kids had always been a part of the picture. He'd known practically from the beginning with Ellie that he wanted those kids with her, and the desire had only strengthened after his friends all started having babies.

But if it was a choice between Ellie and babies…hell, he'd make a great uncle to all the Calloway kids. He could be satisfied with that, as long as he had Ellie.

"Wow." She sank back down on the bed, her head resting on his shoulder. For a time she just lay there, her breathing slow and steady; then she quietly said, "I don't even think of my baby as my daughter. Is that awful?"

He wanted to talk about *their* babies, not the one she'd had with the man she'd loved before him. But it was really part of the same discussion. Her first daughter might have left a big enough hole in her heart that she couldn't bear to have a second.

"No. You gave her parents. She was your baby, but she's their daughter." And though he would have said it anyway, he believed it. Even if it did make him wonder: did his mother still think of him as her son, or was he just the little boy in her past?

"She lives in Marietta. She's got an older brother and a younger sister who are also adopted. She goes to a private school and studies gymnastics and dance and goes to cheerleading camp every summer."

"Have you met her?"

"No. But Randolph Aiken, Andrew's lawyer, knows the family, and he gives me updates if I ask for them." She paused as lightning flashed, then thunder shook the house. When she went on, her tone was resigned. "I don't ask anymore."

Anyone who'd grown up in Georgia knew the Aiken name. They'd owned plantations before the Civil War, had survived the conflict with most of their fortune intact and been quick to expand their business interests after the war. They were the Calloway family on a grander scale.

Which meant that the bastard who had broken Ellie's heart was Andrew Aiken III. He chaired the Aiken Foundation, which seemed to mostly involve handing out checks to worthy charities, hosting fund-raisers and getting his picture taken a lot with celebrities.

I threatened to show up at his family home. Said home being nothing less than a mansion, visited by everyone who was anyone, site of a ball hosted every year by the governor. The idea of his pregnant, seventeen-year-old ex-prostitute mistress inviting herself onto hallowed Aiken ground must have put the fear of God into ol' Andy.

Tommy wished he could have the chance to do the same.

Ellie unfolded his fingers that had clenched into a fist, then clasped his hand in hers. "I never see him, either," she offered. "Oh, on TV, in the papers, in *People,* but it's like seeing a familiar face, someone you can identify but you don't really know."

"You don't still have feelings for him?"

Her chuckle was short. "The last tender feeling I had for Andrew died when I was seven months pregnant and had to beg his uncle for money to keep myself alive long enough to give birth to his baby."

The image was painful. Had Andrew's uncle treated her with respect and human decency? Had he acknowledged that the oh, so privileged Aiken family blood ran through the child whose adoption he was arranging—whose mother he was silencing? Or had he seen Ellie and the baby as just another of his nephew's messes to clean up?

Something nagged at the back of Tommy's mind. Closing his eyes, he took a few deep relaxing breaths, easier to do with her naked and in his arms, and waited for the thought to become clearer. Something about Ellie, the last few days, a phone call...

Friday evening, in the deli, while he'd waited for his to-go order. *Would you please ask Mr. Aiken to call me as soon as he can? He has my numbers...it's really important.*

His muscles tightened as he met her gaze. "Which one of them did you call Friday?"

"Randolph. I wanted to ask his advice—how did you know?"

"I was standing outside your office door, trying to find the courage to either knock or walk away. I heard you leave a message. You've stayed in touch with him all these years?"

She shrugged. "He didn't approve of what Andrew did, or of his own part in it. He knew I needed more than money to get back on my feet, so he helped me find a place in Charleston.

He got me a job. He found the general store and suggested I buy it, and he's given me advice when I ask."

"Does he do that with all of Andrew's exes?"

"I don't know. We never talked about the others." She smiled wryly. "Lawyer-client confidentiality. Scorned-lover disillusionment."

"What advice did you want this time?"

"I was leaving. I wanted him to handle selling the restaurant and the house so…"

So no one from Copper Lake would be in touch with her. Jamie Munroe-Calloway had been Ellie's lawyer since she'd come to town. Had she worried that, client privilege or no, Jamie would give up her location to save Tommy's sanity?

"I would have found you." He said it quietly, a promise. One way or another, legal methods or not, he would have tracked her down. He couldn't have just let her disappear.

"I would have been stunned to think I was worth the effort." So softly that he had to hold his breath to hear, she went on. "All I ever wanted was a normal life. But my parents and fate and circumstance made sure I didn't have that for a long time. I thought I didn't deserve it. But maybe…"

She lifted her gaze to his and said the sweetest words he'd ever heard. Well, second sweetest. He hadn't heard those yet, though he didn't need them to know they were true. *I love you.*

"A baby. Your baby. I like the sound of that."

He couldn't stop the grin that spread across his face. When he'd first fallen in love with her, he'd just assumed that marriage and a family were a given. Then she'd turned down his first proposal, and he had thought that surely she would come around in the near future. Finally he'd realized that the only coming around to be done was by him; he had to accept that she didn't love him, or at least didn't love him enough to marry him and have his kids.

Good things come to those who wait, Pops would say. Tommy had waited long enough.

He lifted himself over her, covering her body with his, pressing his erection against her. "Want to start trying now?" he asked, his mouth brushing hers.

Twining her arms around his neck, she smiled a slow, sexy smile. "I'd like that."

Outside, the storm was intensifying. Inside, the room heated, the air growing heavy and shocky. For the first time since, well, their first time, they made love without a condom, and Tommy found himself hoping that first time would be the charm, just in case she had second thoughts. Not that he would be averse to trying as often as necessary.

Not that he would lose out to second thoughts, or seventieth. They belonged together. End of discussion.

She came first, and that was all he needed to finish. They were lying side by side, their skin and the sheets and the air itself damp with sweat and smelling of sex, when the phone rang. He checked caller ID—the restaurant—and handed the phone to her.

"Hey, Ramona," she greeted. Did the baker hear that she was short of breath? Did she catch that little quaver in Ellie's voice? "Sorry. I'm running a little late this morning."

A little? he mouthed, holding up his wrist so she could see that it was 7:05. She rarely got to the deli later than 6:00 a.m. By the time she showered—again—and dressed—again—she was going to be nearly two hours late.

Leaving her to talk, he went into the bathroom and turned on the water for his second shower. Sweaty and sticky from head to toe, he adjusted the temperature to lukewarm, then stepped under the spray. A few minutes later, the curtain opened and Ellie slipped into the tub with him.

"Any chance you're here to fulfill a few fantasies of mine?"

She smiled at the hopefulness in his voice. In the last six months, he'd hardly ever seen her smiling. It was a really good look for her.

"Ask me again this evening. Ramona's not happy, and I try very hard to keep my staff happy."

"Yeah, you could keep my st—" He broke off when she shot him a look and grinned instead.

She ducked under the spray, letting water stream over her head, turning her hair a shade darker, spiking her lashes, cascading over the perfect lines of her face. She was beautiful. He loved her. And she loved him back.

No matter what else was going on, life was good.

Chapter 10

Though the storm passed within an hour, the rain continued, but it didn't affect business at the deli. During the day, while people were at work, they had to eat lunch somewhere.

At least, that was what Ellie preferred to believe, rather than think the steady business had anything to do with her possible involvement in Martha's death.

Tommy had made a few calls from Ellie's office that morning and located the cemetery in Atlanta where Oliver was buried, and during the morning lull, he'd gone with her to the funeral home to pick out a casket. There would be a graveside service on Friday for any friends Martha might have had, but Ellie hadn't yet decided whether she would go. It seemed wrong of a daughter to stay away from her mother's funeral, no matter how bad the relationship. But at the same time, it struck her as hypocritical to attend, considering the circumstances at the time Martha had died.

Now it was the afternoon lull, and the only customers were in the front dining room. Balancing a tray as easily as she had in her waitressing days, Ellie went into the back room, where Tommy, Robbie and A.J. sat. The table already held four drinks, napkins and sets of silverware. She handed out sandwiches— a Reuben for Robbie, paninis for the rest of them—before sliding into the empty chair.

A cop investigating a murder, one of his suspects, a second cop who was dating said suspect and her defense attorney having lunch and discussing the case. Only in a small town, she thought as she took a bite of roasted veggies, creamy guacamole and mozzarella.

"Do you know if Martha had any ties to Athens?" A.J. asked.

She shook her head.

"Do you have any?"

Underneath the table, Tommy's knee bumped hers. On the way to work, she'd asked him whether anyone else needed to know about her and Andrew. *Don't volunteer it,* he advised, *but don't lie to keep it quiet. Lying makes you look guilty.*

"I know a man there. A lawyer. He helped me get off the streets. Why?"

"We pulled Martha's phone records. There were a dozen or so calls to and from numbers in Athens. She also made two calls there from the Jasmine. All the Athens numbers are pay phones."

A good way, she imagined, to keep calls from being traced back. What was more anonymous than a pay phone?

"She couldn't have called Randolph. He's on an extended vacation to Europe."

A.J. took a bite of his roasted turkey sandwich. "This lawyer…he knows your real name, the name you're using now and where you live?"

Ellie's gut tightened. Randolph Aiken wouldn't have betrayed her. There wasn't a lot she trusted in the world, but she trusted in that.

"He wouldn't be involved with this," she insisted. "He's got too much to lose."

"People will risk just about anything for the right amount of money," Robbie pointed out.

"He doesn't need money."

"How did you choose Ellen Chase for your new name?" A.J. asked after a pause.

Ellie gazed past him to the herb garden out back. The mulch that surrounded each bedraggled plant gleamed in the rain. Everything would look so bright and renewed once the sun came out again, but for now that reddish bark was the only bit of color in a dreary scene.

"Randolph suggested it," she said at last, hating that the answer sounded almost like an indictment against him. "Ellen's parents were clients of his. She had died several years earlier. He had her birth date, her Social Security number, and he helped me get the necessary documents."

"So he betrayed one client to help another," A.J. said.

Though it sounded bad put that way, she emphatically shook her head. "He wouldn't have told Martha anything." Over the years, Randolph had spent a lot of Aiken money as well as his own time and effort to make women like her disappear from Andrew's world. Outing Ellie as Bethany Dempsey increased the risk of exposing Andrew as a two-timing pervert who liked sixteen- and seventeen-year-old girls.

A.J. wasn't convinced, but instead of arguing, he asked, "How do you think Martha found you?"

She'd finished half of her sandwich, but the rest didn't hold much appeal. Pushing the plate away a few inches, she rested her arms in its place and repeated the theories she and Tommy had come up with: that she'd been recognized by a guest from

Jared's birthday party or some long-ago acquaintance who had stopped at the deli on her way through town.

"You've been in the newspaper a few times," Robbie added. "And the deli was featured in that Southern food magazine."

She'd forgotten about that. Good publicity, she'd thought at the time. Besides, neither of her parents had ever read a newspaper or magazine in their lives.

"I'm guessing it was coincidence," she said with a shrug. "Bad luck."

"More for Martha than anyone else," A.J. said drily.

"Payback's a bitch." Tommy's tone was just as dry.

"This lawyer…were you a client or just a social-conscience project?"

A.J. was nothing if not dogged. She sighed. "He never represented me in court, but yes, I was a client."

"Does he have a large practice?"

"I don't know. It appears to be a successful one." Over the years, when she'd called Randolph, she'd spoken to a variety of employees: paralegals, junior lawyers, secretaries and assistants.

Tommy picked up on the direction A.J. was heading. "So there are other people in his office. People who have access to his files, who maybe aren't as ethical or as immune to the lure of easy money."

"I need his name," A.J. demanded.

Ellie gazed at the herb garden again, feeling about as beaten down as the plants looked. When Tommy squeezed her hand reassuringly, her mouth curved up almost enough to be considered a smile. If everything went well, she would be both a wife and a mother before a year was out—two things she hadn't let herself want since Andrew walked out on her.

If things didn't go well, if District Attorney Tatum decided the state's case was strong enough, she'd be in prison before a year was out. And considering that she had motive, means and opportunity, to say nothing of nine missing hours, A.J.'s doubts wouldn't count for much with Tatum unless he could serve up another suspect with an even stronger case.

"Randolph Aiken," she said at last.

Robbie clearly recognized the name, his gaze narrowing suspiciously. A.J. didn't look as if it meant a thing to him, but no doubt, soon after he got back to his office, he would know more about Randolph than she did. He wasn't the type to do his job carelessly.

Lucky for her.

A.J. swigged down the last of his tea, then rose. "Got a check?"

She waved her free hand. "It's on the house."

"No, thanks," he said as pleasantly as if saying *thank you.*

She often gave cops and sheriff's deputies free food, but with A.J. investigating her, she supposed it really wasn't proper. "Sherry will write it up for you at the front."

He left with a curt nod, and silence fell over the table. Robbie finally broke it, his voice cautious. "I'm guessing if you know Randolph Aiken that you might have met him through his nephew."

Ellie's face flushed, making her long for just a moment to step out into the rain to cool down.

"You know about him?" Tommy asked hostilely.

Robbie shrugged. "From years ago. There were rumors, but none of the girls ever came forward, and Aiken damn sure never admitted anything. Story was that the family paid them to forget his name."

Ellie confirmed it with a nod. How many others had there been? Enough for people to gossip about. Fewer than five? More than ten? Had they all been pregnant, or had simple seduction been enough to warrant Randolph's intervention?

"If your mother's information did come from someone in

Aiken's office, there may be other blackmail victims out there," Robbie said.

Other girls who'd fallen for Andrew's pretty face and prettier words, girls who'd been hungry and scared and desperate to believe someone wanted them. Whose silence had been bought, whose babies had been traded for the money to survive, whose secrets were now being threatened. Ellie knew Randolph would never stoop so low. But someone who worked for him? They were total strangers to her. One of them could easily be the type to threaten to destroy another person's life for money. Her own mother had been.

Tommy's fingers tightened around hers. "Jesus." He sounded dismayed. He was part cynic—after six or eight months on the job, all cops developed a cynical streak, he said—but she knew there was a part of him, even after all he'd seen, that still thought a small measure of decency wasn't too much to ask of anyone.

After all she'd seen, she knew it was. But she loved him for still expecting to find good in people. For finding it in her.

"What happens now?" she asked.

It was Tommy who grudgingly answered, "Decker will confirm that Aiken's out of the country. He'll track him down, get a list of employees, check them out, try to find out about any other clients worth blackmailing."

Robbie snorted. "Probably everyone he's ever represented."

"And what do we do?" Ellie knew the answer before the men exchanged glances.

"We wait," Tommy said simply.

Another silence settled, this one hanging heavy until footsteps sounded in the corridor. Anamaria came around the corner, smiling brightly when she saw them. She looked radiant and gave off warmth and the subtle scent of cinnamon when she hugged Ellie.

She bent to embrace Tommy from behind, then gave the

biggest hug to her husband before settling in the empty chair. Her gaze shifted between Ellie and Tommy and their clasped hands. "You two are good."

It wasn't a question, but Ellie nodded anyway. She didn't even consider telling her best friend that Tommy wanted to marry her, or that she wanted to marry him back. Some news needed to be savored a little before going public.

"Yeah," she said, turning to find Tommy watching her. "We're very good."

When the staff tried to send Ellie home before dinner, she refused to go, and she didn't hide in her office, either. Tommy sat at a corner table, watching her move seemingly without effort through her usual routine: chatting with diners, refilling glasses and coffee cups, cashing out checks and seating newcomers. He could see the tension in her, though, probably because studying her had been his favorite pastime for five years. Every time she felt a curious gaze lingering on her, her spine stiffened, and each time a table of diners stopped talking abruptly as she approached, something flashed in her eyes.

He hoped she noticed, though, that the majority of diners were there for dinner, nothing more.

One who wasn't was Louise Wetherby. Her restaurant down the street might have class, Anamaria said, but Louise did not. She sat at the table next to Tommy's with her husband, a meek man who rarely spoke or made eye contact with anyone, including his wife.

Ellie had left the dining room when Louise turned her attention to him. "Are you on duty, Detective?"

"No, ma'am."

Her gaze flicked from him to the table, empty except for a glass of tea, then back. "You're spending your evening off in the restaurant owned by the woman suspected of killing Martha

Dempsey, not dining and watching Ellie Chase like a hawk, but you're not working. Uh-huh."

The wise thing was to ignore her, and he did, letting his gaze drift around the room as he took a drink.

But Louise Wetherby didn't like being ignored. "It's such a shame. Martha was a lovely woman. Such a loss."

He choked on his tea, coughing and sputtering. So much for ignoring her. "A lovely woman? Martha Dempsey? Gray hair, heavy smoker, mean eyes?"

Louise got huffy. "It's rude to speak poorly of the dead. I found Martha to be a charming, intelligent woman."

She wouldn't know charm if it bit her on the ass, Tommy thought. Intelligence, either.

Louise's own mean little eyes narrowed. "You used to be involved with Ellie Chase, didn't you?" The way she said *involved* sounded as if they'd made a habit of having wild sex on the courthouse steps. "Are you together again? Are you foolish enough to believe that she didn't run down that poor woman in the street? Why, I heard from Benton Tatum just today that it's only a matter of time before he charges her. And how will that look for you, Detective, having your girlfriend in prison?"

His jaw tightened. "She hasn't been arrested yet, and she won't be convicted."

"You sound so sure of that. Why? Because she has an in with the police department? Because you're going to see to it that something happens to the evi—"

Across the room, the door opened and Decker walked in. Tommy shoved to his feet and walked away from Louise in midrant.

"Rude young man," she said loudly enough to carry. "I'll certainly be complaining to the chief about this."

"The old hag complains so much that the chief panics if you

just say her name around him," Decker said quietly. "Can we talk in Ellie's office?"

"Sure." Tommy led the way down the hall, swinging the door open and switching on the light.

"Doesn't she ever lock the door?"

"Only if she's, uh, occupied." Like the rare occasions when the two of them had put the couch to good use. It had been a long time since they'd done that, though. "According to Louise, the D.A. says he's planning to charge Ellie. Have you heard?"

"It's an election year. Tatum wants to appear tough on crime."

Which meant, yes, Decker had heard it. Tommy's gut tightened. He *knew* Ellie was innocent. He also knew innocence was no protection against arrest, trial and conviction. If she had to go to trial…God help them, if she had to go to prison…how could either of them stand that?

"I talked to Aiken," Decker went on. "Nice guy, considering it was two in the morning over there. He's been in Europe for a month and will be there six more weeks. Making up to the wife for all the trips they didn't take while he was still working."

It took a minute for his last words to sink in. Tommy frowned. "You mean, he's retired?"

"Pretty much. His staff has all gone on to other jobs except for one. Marie Jensen. She's his secretary. Been with him for twenty-some years. She's transferring records to other lawyers, getting everything on computer for storage, closing up the office. She's fifty-two. Divorced. No kids. She lives alone but spends a lot of time at the nursing home where her mother lives. Never been arrested, doesn't have anything unusual on her credit history, no more money in the bank than you'd expect, goes to church on Sundays. She doesn't have a new job lined up yet. She's considering her options."

Tommy adjusted the window blinds so he could see out, though the only view was the brick wall of the building next door and, overhead, the night sky. "Have any of his other clients had any problems?"

"Not that he knows of, but like I said, he's been gone a month. The only way most of them have to contact him is his office."

"Where Marie is answering calls and taking messages." Tommy rubbed between his eyes where a headache was trying to start. "What's his gut instinct about her?"

"That she couldn't be involved in something like this."

"What's yours?"

"He never would have kept her on if he hadn't trusted her fully. But you and I both know that a lot of bad guys are capable of hiding their true nature. People see what they want them to see. And she could have been fully trustworthy until something happened. Maybe her mother's care is overwhelming her. Maybe the idea of starting over at a new job at her age is too much. Maybe she's been tempted all along and finally gave in."

Desperation could make a person do things she never would have considered. Ellie was proof of that. But it was a big step from blackmail to murder. Most blackmailers weren't violent. Desperation again: fear of getting caught, reluctance to go to prison, leaving her mother alone. And when she had the perfect suspect in her partner's daughter…

Tommy turned away from the window and leaned against the sill. "When did Martha make the two calls from the Jasmine?"

"Wednesday evening around six-fifteen and Saturday morning. Ten forty-two."

A few hours before she'd confronted Ellie for the first time and again before she'd issued her demand for an answer the next day.

"Did Aiken mention that Ellie had left a couple of messages for him?"

"No. Said he hasn't talked to her in eight or ten months."

"Did he say when he last spoke to Marie?"

"Every Monday morning, our time, since he left, and again on Thursdays. She gives him messages, he tells her what to do."

"Ellie left messages for him last Friday. Said it was really important."

"Wonder why Jensen didn't tell him," Decker said sardonically as he pulled a paper folded in quarters from his pocket. "I got this from Drivers Services. Look familiar?"

Tommy smoothed the folds, then studied the photograph of Aiken's secretary. She looked her age, pleasant, fairly unremarkable. Her hair was too perfectly blond to be natural, her cheeks plump, her smile warm.

Had she been at the Halloween festival? He had no clue. But then, he had spent most of the evening watching Ellie, and there'd been more than a few witches there. "If I saw her, I don't remember."

"Forgettable is the best way for crooks to look."

"Okay, so Marie Jensen knows her boss is retiring. It's her last chance to fatten up her own retirement plan. She knows about—" Tommy broke off abruptly. He'd been about to say *the nephew's girlfriends*. If the secretary was the blackmailer, it would all come out in the end, but until then, he wouldn't break Ellie's confidence. "She knows Ellie doesn't want her past coming out, so she recruits Martha for her blackmail. Why use a partner? Why not approach Ellie directly?"

Decker sprawled on the sofa, legs stretched out, ankles crossed over a rung on the chair that fronted the desk. "An extra layer of protection between her and the crime. I bet Martha didn't have an idea in hell who she was dealing with. As far as Ellie knew, as far as *we* know for sure, Martha was acting alone. She could have talked about her partner until she was blue in the face, but she wouldn't have had a name or a face to put to her, nothing but a bunch of pay phones to point to as proof."

"Assuming Ellie's not the only target, Jensen picks people who are greedy enough to be the face guy but who can't ID her. She provides the material, they approach the target and she splits the money with them, all the time staying anonymous to everyone."

Decker nodded in agreement.

"So why kill Martha?"

"You said Ellie called Aiken Friday afternoon. Says it's important—she needs to talk to him right away. Jensen thinks Ellie's going to tell him about the blackmail. She can't risk the boss finding out that Ellie's not the only client being targeted, so she comes to Copper Lake, kills Martha, removing the only possible link between herself and the blackmail, and, as a bonus, she frames Ellie. She has to know that we're going to find out pretty quick that Ellie isn't who she says she is, and then we're going to find out her criminal history. Desperate people do desperate things."

Less than thirty hours had passed between Ellie's phone calls to Aiken and Martha's death. Not a lot of time to plan a murder and a frame. But as murders went, hit-and-run was fairly simple. The most difficult part of the plan would have been getting her hands on the drug, and even that wouldn't have been tough for a resourceful woman. She lived in a college town and had worked half her life for a criminal-defense attorney. She had access to people who had access to just about anything.

"I wonder if she's blackmailed other clients," Tommy said.

"I wonder if she's killed other partners."

The thought made Tommy stiffen. They could be talking not about a woman desperate for money, but a cold-blooded murderer. Killing Martha might have been her plan all along; she'd just been forced to do it before the payoff this time because of Ellie's attempt to contact Aiken.

Decker was thinking along the same lines. "Since Ellie's calls made Jensen act before, let's have her call again. Tell her she *has* to talk to Aiken, that she's found out things he's got to know."

"And she'll reach him some other way if Jensen can't get hold of him." The secretary would buy that. After all, she knew about Ellie and her boss's nephew.

"If she is the guilty one, she'll come here to get rid of Ellie, just like she got rid of Martha."

Set up Ellie as a target for murder. Tommy's hands were clammy, and acid churned in his gut. Set up the woman he loved to let some psychopath try to kill her. He wanted to object, to say no way, but the choice wasn't really his; it was Ellie's. And if they were prepared, if everything went right, her name would be cleared and there would be no threat of arrest, trial or prison.

But if something went wrong...

No way. But those weren't the words that came out when he finally got enough breath to power his voice.

"Let's talk to her."

It was nine-thirty Wednesday morning. The sun was shining, and the air had a bit of a fall nip, just enough to remind a person that winter, such as it was, was coming. If Ellie had her way, she would be outside at that very moment, strolling through the square, maybe stopping in at A Cuppa Joe for hot cocoa, tapping on the window of Jamie's office to wave hello or admiring River's Edge with its autumn-hued mums and pansies.

She wouldn't be sitting in her office, surrounded by grim-faced men. She wouldn't be jittery and anxious, and she definitely wouldn't be about to make a phone call that might result in an attempt on her life.

Tommy was leaning against the wall behind her chair, his pose relaxed, but she could feel the tension vibrating around him. He'd been noncommittal about this phone call. He'd made certain she understood the risks, and he'd promised she would be safe, but he hadn't tried to persuade or dissuade her. He'd trusted her judgment to make the right choice.

She hoped she had.

Robbie sat on the couch, and A.J. was in the visitor chair. A fourth man by the name of Galvez was finishing up his job of wiring the phone to record the call. When he was done, he nodded, and she picked up the phone, her hand trembling a bit as she dialed.

A woman answered on the second ring. "Aiken Law Office. This is Marie."

"Hello, Marie, this is Ellie Chase. I called last week trying to get hold of Mr. Aiken?"

"Oh, yes, Miss Chase. I'm sorry. Has he not called you back yet?"

"No, he hasn't, and it's really urgent that I speak to him. I really don't want to go into detail, but I, uh, found out something that he really needs to know. It could be terribly damaging to him and everyone who works for him."

There was a moment's silence; then, confidence strong in her voice, Marie said, "You can tell me anything, Miss Chase. I've been Mr. Aiken's right hand for twenty-seven years now. I know everything that goes on in this office. And if I know what the problem is, I can be sure it's presented with the importance it deserves." A phony little laugh. "You'd be surprised what some of our clients consider urgent. A parking ticket, an ex being a day late with his child support, a daughter getting suspended for one day from middle school. Not that I'm trivializing your problem, but you understand, it's my job to prioritize Mr. Aiken's calls so I'm not bothering him halfway around the world with truly minor issues."

"Well…" Ellie wrapped the phone cord around one finger. "I hate to make accusations, but…I think someone who works for him is blackmailing me."

There was utter silence for a few seconds; then Marie, sounding hollow, said, "Oh my God. Of course I'll contact Mr.

Aiken right away. It may take a while. He's traveling, you know, and there's the time difference, and cell service isn't always reliable. But I'll get your message to him and—"

Ellie interrupted. "You know, Marie, I shouldn't have involved you in this. After all, these people are your friends and coworkers. I'll just call Mr. Aiken myself. We've got some mutual friends. I can get his cell number from one of them, and if not, there's always Andrew. I'm sure he would be happy to help once he knows what's going on."

Another brief silence, then urgency: "Please don't do that, Miss Chase. I'll reach Mr. Aiken, and he'll call you right away. I promise."

"Thank you, Marie." Ellie hung up and wiped her sweaty palms on a napkin printed with Ellie's Deli.

"Who is Andrew?" A.J. asked as Galvez dismantled the equipment.

"Randolph's nephew." Deliberately misleading the detective, she glanced at Robbie. "It helps to know people who know people." Let him assume that her knowledge of one rich lawyer's family came through another rich lawyer.

"I've got a friend in Athens keeping an eye on Jensen. If she leaves, he'll let us know."

"You have friends everywhere, don't you?" she asked, trying to ease a little of the tension in the room.

A.J.'s shrug was accompanied by what might have been the beginnings of a smile if it hadn't faded so fast. "Did her voice seem at all familiar?"

Ellie shook her head. She'd listened hard, but any recognition more likely would have been from talking to the woman on the phone last Friday, not in the bar on Saturday. She'd studied the photograph of Marie Jensen the day before, but had drawn a blank there, too.

"Petrovski's out back, and DeLong's out front," A.J. went

on. "Don't set foot out of this building without one of them or Maricci, understand?"

"She's not going anywhere," Tommy said from behind her, and she felt no need to disagree. She could stay here in the deli, with both doors guarded, for days if necessary.

She could stay with Tommy forever.

As the conversation went on around her, she stared at the crumpled napkin, unable to focus on it. Marie Jensen was, by all accounts, an ordinary woman. She'd had a good job and made a comfortable life for herself and, in recent years, her mother, and yet she'd dug through her boss's files to locate people who were vulnerable, to use their misfortunes for her gain. After half a century of ordinariness, she'd turned to crime, to betrayal and murder.

Ellie could more easily understand Martha's greed. Oliver had never been a great provider, but in the last few months without him, she'd seen that a tough life was about to get tougher. No doubt, she'd really believed that Ellie owed her; she'd justified her actions as merely claiming what was rightfully hers.

But Marie Jensen didn't need Ellie's money to survive. A.J. had told her Marie owned a nice house and a two-year-old car. She took vacations twice a year and had money in savings and in a retirement plan. She didn't know Ellie, as Martha had. She didn't hate her, as Martha had.

And yet she was willing to destroy Ellie—first, for money; now, if Tommy and A.J.'s theory was correct, to cover up her crimes.

What turned an ordinary woman into a killer?

If the guys' theory was correct, she might get the chance to ask the woman herself.

Less than an hour after everyone cleared out of her office, A.J. called Tommy with the news that Marie Jensen had, indeed, left her office soon after the phone call. His friend had followed her to the post office and the bank before losing her inside the mall. He'd returned to watch her car, but after three hours with no sign of her, the consensus was that she'd left by some other means.

The news made Tommy look grim and heightened Ellie's queasiness, even though every cop in town had Marie's description. There were officers stationed outside the deli's doors, and Tommy was never more than a shout away. She was safe.

The hours dragged past. Business was better than good— they served lunch to two buses of senior citizens who'd driven over from Augusta to tour Calloway Plantation and River's Edge—but she just wanted the day to be over. She wanted to go home, curl up in bed next to Tommy and sleep as if she didn't have a care in the world.

She wanted all of this to be over and done.

As long as she came out of it alive and free.

"You look tired. Why don't you go home? I'll close up for you."

Ellie smiled faintly at Carmen. It wasn't even seven yet, but the assistant manager looked tired, too. With all that had happened, she'd come in early the last three days and stayed late the last two nights so Ellie wouldn't have to. Working the extra hours, along with caring for her five children, was obviously starting to wear on her. "Thanks, but I think it's your turn to cut out. Go home to your family."

"They can take care of themselves for another night."

"Go on," Ellie urged. "I bet you haven't even seen the kids awake since Sunday."

"You say that as if it's a bad thing," Carmen retorted with a smirk. "Are you sure you wouldn't rather get out of here?"

"I'm sure." As much as she'd like to be home in bed with Tommy, it wasn't as if she would feel any more relaxed at home; she might as well be antsy here and give Carmen a break.

"Well, if you're certain," Carmen said, already heading toward the kitchen.

Ellie waited tables, helped in the kitchen and ordered supplies. She posted the work schedule for the next week; then, with Tommy's help, she shut down the back dining room at eight, wiped the tables, refilled the salt and pepper shakers and mopped up. The whole time she couldn't help wondering if Marie Jensen was out there in the dark, watching through the windows that stretched across the room, or if she'd decided, as Ellie herself had a few days ago, to cut her losses and run.

"Petrovski's out there."

Ellie saw Tommy's reflection in the glass a moment before he bumped against her from behind. She leaned into him, taking comfort in his warmth and solidness. "Poor guy. It's been a long day."

"He got a two-hour break, and he volunteered for the overtime."

She gazed at their image for a moment, then into the darkness of the herb garden. "Where do you think she is?"

"Don't have a clue. Maybe on the first plane to Rio."

"Or maybe here in town."

He nodded once, his chin bumping her head. "Maybe," he agreed. "Any chance you've changed your mind about bunking in a jail cell?"

"I've been in jail more times than you want to know. I don't want to go back."

"Not even for your own safety?"

"I'm safe with you."

He exaggerated his usual Southern drawl. "I'm honored by your faith in me."

Not as honored as she was by his love for her, she thought with a faint smile as she went back to work.

At eight forty-five the last diners left. At nine o'clock, the front door was locked and by nine-fifteen, the last of the staff had departed by the rear door. Ellie and Tommy worked together, cleaning the main dining room, the bar, the bath-rooms. All that was left was preparing the bank deposit. She'd just settled at her desk to start that when his cell phone rang.

He greeted A.J., and her nerves tightened. When he swore, her fingers clenched the ink pen tightly enough to make them numb. "Let me know," he said curtly before disconnecting.

"Bad news?"

"They had a disturbance call to Stormy's Tavern. Shots fired, a number of people down, including two officers." His mouth tightening, he dragged his fingers through his hair.

"You should go."

"They don't need me."

"But you need to be there."

Shaking his head, he jumped to his feet and paced the length of the room, agitation rolling off him in waves. Officer-down calls were the worst, he'd told her before. He didn't just work with these people; they were friends, partners, brothers on the job.

She laid the pen on top of a stack of twenties and moved to block his path. Outside, sirens wailed, increasing as emergency vehicles came nearer, then fading as they raced on past. "Tommy, we're the only two here. Pete Petrovski is still out back. Someone else is out front. The place is locked up tight. I couldn't be safer. Go help where you're needed."

He hesitated, clearly torn, then abruptly kissed her. "I'll be back."

"I'll be waiting."

Spinning around, he left the office, his footsteps sounding oddly hollow in the quiet restaurant. The front door creaked, better than a bell at announcing customers, and the murmur of Tommy's conversation with the officer silhouetted in the open doorway filtered back to where she stood. Apparently satisfied that all was well at the front, he secured the door, passed her again with a gentle touch, then went into the kitchen. A moment later, the back door closed with a thud, and she was truly alone for the first time in four days.

This place is spooky when it's empty, he'd said Monday morning, and she'd disagreed. From the moment she'd walked through the front door that first day five years ago, she'd known she and this building were meant for each other. It was a symbol of how far she'd come. She felt at home there.

But it was just a little spooky tonight, she decided as she closed the office door, locked it, then returned to her desk.

An occasional siren passed as she counted out cash and coins, totaled checks and organized credit card receipts, and she said a quick prayer between tasks. It had been a very good day for the business; she was long past the point where she could turn over much of the day-to-day responsibilities to someone else and take time for herself. Spend time with friends. With Tommy.

With family.

She slid the cash into a locking bank bag and zipped it shut as a noise sounded from the rear of the building. Instinctively she started, then realized Tommy must have forgotten something; he hadn't been gone long enough to reach the bar on the east edge of town, and Pete wouldn't let just anyone enter.

Leaving the bag on the desk, she crossed to the door and twisted the lock. "That was quick. Is everything—"

It wasn't Tommy who stood in the hallway, face shadowed by the dim lights burning there and in the bar. The woman was about her height, though considerably heavier, and looked old enough to be harmless.

The question of harmless didn't apply to the pistol she carried.

"Hello, Ellie. Do you mind if I come in?"

Ellie backed away, and Marie Jensen advanced, closing the door behind her. Her disguise was a good one: gray wig; heavy makeup that gave her an aged, sallow look; dumpy shirt and pants; ugly shoes. Except for the thin latex gloves she wore, she looked like someone's frumpy grandma.

"How did you get past the officers outside?"

"Oh, I've been here awhile, upstairs in that private room. I walked in the front door, right past you and that cute little detective boyfriend of yours, and neither of you ever looked twice at me."

The tour group, Ellie realized. There had been a few men, but mostly it had been made up of women ranging from every-hair-in-place to majorly frumpy. She would have fit right in.

"You couldn't have known when you chose your disguise that we would have sixty-eight seniors here for lunch," Ellie commented, surprised that her voice was steady.

"A happy coincidence. I love those. Don't you?"

"The officer-down call from the bar…was that another coincidence? Or did you make it?"

"'This is Josie out at Stormy's Tavern. Someone's shootin' up the parkin' lot,'" Marie said, her voice coarse, her accent thick. "'There's people lying all over the place, and God Almighty, I think them two cops are dead.'" She smirked. "I used to do community theater. I'm very good with makeup and dialects."

Ellie kept her gaze locked on Marie while doing a frantic mental search for a way out. Marie blocked the door. The windows were big enough to crawl through, but they'd been painted shut since before Ellie had moved in. The glass had been in them decades longer, two panes sandwiching wire mesh. Tough to break out.

Choices for weapons were limited, as well: a lamp near the sofa, another on the desk, the telephone. Where was a heavy silver candlestick when you needed one? Or a strong, experienced cop?

I'll be back.

And she would be waiting, she'd told Tommy. Alive, she now hoped.

Knees weakened by the alternative, she sank into the chair behind the desk. What was in the drawers? Pens, paper clips, a stapler. No letter opener; she preferred to tear the flap. A pair of scissors with two-inch round-tipped blades, not likely to do any real damage. Files, a thin Copper Lake phone book.

Heavy glasses and bottles in the bar, knives and rolling pins and skillets in the kitchen. Makeshift weapons everywhere but here.

"Why did you pick me?" The quaver that had made her legs unsteady had traveled up into her voice now.

"You fit my requirements." Marie ticked them off on her fingers. "Having the truth come out was your greatest fear. I wanted money. You had it. I had the truth." With a shrug as if it were truly that simple, she slid a bag off her shoulder onto the visitor chair. She lined up its contents on the far edge of the desk: a bottle of wine, likely taken from the bar; a glass; a coffee stirrer; a pill bottle half filled with powder; a manila file folder; and a sheet of paper. "Why don't you get some paper and copy this note in your own handwriting."

Slowly Ellie removed a notepad from the drawer, an ink pen from another and slid Marie's note closer.

My real name is Bethany Dempsey. Martha Dempsey was my mother. I'd hidden from her for fifteen years, but she found me and threatened to destroy my new life if I didn't give her everything. I couldn't do it. I'd worked too hard, and I hated her too much. So I killed her.

I thought it would be easy. It was only fair, after everything she'd done to me. I didn't expect to feel guilty. Just relieved. But I can't stand it. I can't stand what she turned me into. I can't stand everyone knowing the truth about me.

I'm sorry. I'm so sorry.

"I can't write this," Ellie said quietly.

Marie set the pistol on the chair seat, well out of reach, and opened the pill bottle. The white powder inside was ground-up pills, Ellie realized, to help speed their action. Marie dumped a large dose of the powder into the wineglass, then filled the glass two-thirds, stirring it until the powder dissolved.

Then she looked at Ellie. "You have two options, and walking out of here isn't one of them. You can copy that note and drink this wine, go to sleep and never wake up, or you can copy the note and blow your brains out. Keep in mind that it's probably your boyfriend who will find you. Do you want him to find you resting in peace? Or a bloody mess?"

Ellie glanced at the wine, a pretty, deep red, showing no sign of the fine powder dissolved in it. She had to believe she could stall long enough, that Tommy would realize something was wrong, that he would know she needed him.

But what if he didn't get back in time? Which would haunt him less: an overdose? Or a gunshot to the head?

That's a no-brainer, she could hear him saying with that dry dark humor that got him through the tough times at work.

Still, she couldn't make herself pick up the glass. She reached for it, but her hand trembled too badly. She clasped her fingers tightly together. "You'll never get away—"

Marie swiftly raised the gun, the barrel cold and hard against Ellie's temple. She pressed just hard enough to make it bite into the skin. "You're not walking out of here, Ellie." Her voice was calm, oddly pleasant, sending a shiver through Ellie. "I've got too much invested here. Too much to lose. Start. Drinking. Now."

Ellie's breath came, quick and shallow, but she couldn't move. Couldn't reach for the glass. Couldn't lift the pen.

Then Marie drew back the hammer, not much more than a click, but the most frightening sound Ellie had ever heard. The ice holding her motionless shattered and she picked up the glass, sloshing droplets over her fingers as she raised it to her mouth and sipped.

The pressure of the gun barrel against her temple didn't ease until the third drink. Slowly Marie withdrew, eased the hammer down again, then looked around the office. "Keep drinking and start writing. Where do you keep your important papers?"

"There's a safe in the credenza." Ellie gestured toward the built-in piece behind her, sipped more wine, then picked up the ink pen. *My real name is Bethany Dempsey.*

Marie took the folder—and the gun, Ellie saw with disappointment—to the credenza and opened doors until she found the hidden safe. "Combination?"

Swiveling to face her, Ellie rattled off the numbers. A few edges stuck out of the folder, enough to recognize the pages: arrest reports. It was the original of the file she'd burned in her fireplace a week ago, the original A.J. hadn't been able to find among Martha's belongings.

Marie skimmed over the items in the safe, nothing of value to her, then tossed the folder on top. For good measure, she sprinkled a little powder from the pill bottle inside, too, before closing the door and spinning the lock. "Drink. Write."

Sip. *Martha Dempsey was my mother.* "Why did you kill her?"

"She was greedy and stupid. I told her to get the cash and get out, but she decided she wanted to stay here and be taken care of. She made you suspicious enough to call Randolph. Most blackmail victims are smart enough to keep their mouths shut and pay up as soon as they can get the cash together. But not you. No, you have to call your damned lawyer."

Ellie tried to focus on the line she was writing. She was so tired. Probably the wine on top of a long, stressful day. Then the desire to giggle hit her: the wine was laced with enough sedative to kill her. Yep, that could make her tired.

Her eyes were drooping shut when pain lanced through her

scalp. Holding a handful of Ellie's hair, Marie gave her head a vicious shake. "Finish the damn letter."

Drink. *I didn't expect to feel guilty.*

"Tommy will never believe..." The letters swayed on the paper, and she blinked to hold them steady. "He'll never believe..." Something important, but what?

Marie snorted. "He'll have your suicide note written in your own hand. Your fingerprints will be on the wine bottle and the glass. The file covered with Martha's fingerprints is in your safe. It may break his heart, but he'll believe."

Break his heart. She'd done that before. Wouldn't ever do it again. Loved him. More than she'd ever loved...

Another drink, another line.

Last drink. Last line. It was a struggle, holding her head up, keeping her eyes open, maintaining a grip on the pen, making it move in legible lines. *I'm sorry. I'm sorrysorrysor*

Stormy's Tavern was located a mile and a half outside the town proper, just fifty feet inside the city limits. Long before the bar's neon lights came into sight, the road, narrowed to two lanes, became clogged with passersby and emergency vehicles casting a ghostly blue and red glow into the air.

Waiting for a chance to pull into the parking lot, Tommy stared at the scene. There were a lot of people milling around: customers, employees, curious neighbors, emergency personnel. Voices carrying through the open window hummed with excitement, but there was little activity. Paramedics and firemen stood in small groups talking. Most of the cops were making a halfhearted effort at crowd and traffic control, but there was no sense of urgency, no shock, no adrenaline rushing.

No victims' bodies lying on the parking lot.

There'd been no shooting.

Damn!

Spinning the steering wheel in a tight circle, Tommy gunned the engine, shooting across the lane in front of oncoming traffic. The SUV rocked when the right wheels went off the pavement, then again when they regained traction.

A damned diversion. Every cop on duty or off would respond to an officer-down call, leaving the entire rest of the town pretty much empty. It was easier to take out one or two cops when backup was at least eight or ten minutes away.

He raced back toward the center of town, veering into the opposite lane to pass slower-moving vehicles, jamming the brakes when he couldn't pass. His tires squealed through the turn onto River Road, and the SUV bumped over the curb when he cut it short angling into the alley. He skidded to a stop at the foot of the deli's rear steps and jumped out of the truck before the engine died.

In the shadows at the end of the lot, a car door opened and Petrovski climbed out. "Hey, Maricci, everything okay?"

"Have you seen anything?"

"No, it's been quiet. What about—"

"The shooting call was bogus. Find Gadney around front. Make sure everything's okay there." As Petrovski reached for his police radio, Tommy unlocked the door and stepped inside.

The deli was quiet, the same lights on as when he'd left. He slid his gun from its holster, then moved silently through the shadowy kitchen and into the broad hallway. Light shone from underneath the office door. Nothing appeared out of place.

He eased up against the wall, reaching for the doorknob. If he was overreacting, he was going to scare the hell out of Ellie. But the hairs standing on end on the back of his neck and the tightness in his gut were pretty good indicators that he wasn't overreacting. Something *felt* wrong.

Before his fingers closed around the knob, it turned from the inside and the door opened. He jerked back, flat against the wall, as a woman came out. She carried a tote bag and was dressed in jeans and one of the Ellie's Deli T-shirts the wait-staff wore. Her hair was red, and she wore oversize glasses that gave her a bug-eyed look. Together with the wig, they took ten years off her age, but he knew that face. He'd been staring at a picture of it off and on all day.

He extended his arm, gun pointing directly at Marie Jensen, and stepped out of the shadows. She whirled around, her own arm extended, her own gun aimed at him.

Too late, he thought in a panic, but he didn't dare take his gaze from her to look inside the room for Ellie.

Marie's smile was as cold and empty as her eyes, at odds with her warm drawl. "You're too late, Detective. Poor Ellie. So troubled over what she's done."

Fear surged inside him, but his hand remained steady. "Put the gun down, Marie."

"I can't do that."

"You don't have a choice."

She smiled again. "A person always has choices, Detective." Her finger tightened on the trigger, and a curious look came into her eyes. Triumph, maybe.

The shot was deafening in the contained space. Her body spun backward into the doorway of the bar, landing facedown on the wood floor. The gun was still in her grip, her finger still on the trigger, but it was too late to pull it.

Tommy stared at her only an instant. He didn't have to go closer, didn't have to check to know she was dead. A .45-caliber bullet to the chest at close range...

Footsteps pounding into the kitchen nearly obscured the whisper of sound from the office. Tommy spun around and bolted into the room.

Ellie sat slumped at her desk, her hair hiding her face, one arm dangling at her side. A wine bottle lay beneath her fingers, red wine gurgling out, spreading across the desktop.

"Ellie?" *Oh God, oh God.* He found her pulse, thready, slowing even as he checked. "Get your car, Pete!" he yelled as he lifted her into his arms, then shoved the chair out of the way and headed toward the hall, where Petrovski was staring, green around the gills, at Jensen. "Move! We've got to get her to the hospital."

"Oh, man, it's too late," Petrovski said, then did a double take when he saw Ellie. He dashed into the kitchen and out the back door, and Tommy followed.

It wasn't too late. He wouldn't let it be. He couldn't let it be.

He prayed all the way to the hospital. *Oh God, oh God, oh God.*

Friday afternoon was sunny and warm, the sky an incredible blue. Ellie stood next to a casket the color of ancient pewter, a single red rose in her hand. She hadn't thought to get flowers, but Sara Calloway and her daughters-in-law had ordered them; so had Tommy's father and Pops.

The three Calloway boys and their wives stood some distance back, giving her privacy. She'd been surprised that they would attend; after all, they hadn't known Martha. *But we know you,* Anamaria had said. *We'll be there for you.*

Tommy had offered to wait with them, but Ellie had clasped his hand instead. She had lost consciousness Wednesday night thinking she would never see him again. She needed him near.

"I didn't love her," she remarked.

"She gave you no reason to."

And so many reasons not to. "She was a poor excuse for a mother."

"But she was your mother."

And Ellie had wanted to do what daughters did when their mothers died: bury her. Show a moment's respect for the relationship that might have been.

Promise herself that her own mother/child relationships would be exactly what they should.

With a sigh, she laid the rose on the casket, then glanced around. Martha was dead, and no one truly mourned. Marie Jensen was dead. Randolph Aiken was on his way home to, once again, clean up someone else's messes. He'd already located two other blackmail victims among his former clients. Likely there were more.

What terrible events Martha had set in motion when she'd thrown her teenage daughter out of the house fifteen years ago.

Tommy's free hand, warm and solid, brushed her cheek. "Are you all right?"

Ellie drew a deep breath, smelling flowers, fresh earth and autumn leaves, then smiled at him. "I'm better than all right." A pause. "Are you?"

He'd shot suspects twice before, but neither had died. He was pragmatic about it, though. If he hadn't killed Marie, she would have killed him. If her dying meant his living, it was a better-than-fair trade.

"Yeah. I am."

She smiled again, awed by the pure pleasure of looking at him, touching him, talking to him. "I love you, you know."

His grin was slow, brash and endearing as he slid his arm around her shoulders and began walking with her to where their friends waited. "I know, darlin'. I've always known. I've just been waiting for you to figure it out."

* * * * *

*Celebrate 60 years of pure reading pleasure
with Harlequin®!*

To commemorate the event, Silhouette Special Edition
invites you to Ashley O'Ballivan's bed-and-breakfast in
the small town of Stone Creek. The beautiful innkeeper
will have her hands full caring for her old flame Jack
McCall. He's on the run and recovering from a mysteri-
ous illness, but that won't stop him from trying to win
Ashley back.

*Enjoy an exclusive glimpse of Linda Lael Miller's
AT HOME IN STONE CREEK.
Available in November 2009 from
Silhouette Special Edition®.*

The helicopter swung abruptly sideways in a dizzying arch, setting Jack McCall's fever-ravaged brain spinning.

His friend's voice sounded tinny, coming through the earphones. "You belong in a hospital," he said. "Not some backwater bed-and-breakfast."

All Jack really knew about the virus raging through his system was that it wasn't contagious, and there was no known treatment for it besides a lot of rest and quiet. "I don't like hospitals," he responded, hoping he sounded like his normal self. "They're full of sick people."

Vince Griffin chuckled but it was a dry sound, rough at the edges. "What's in Stone Creek, Arizona?" he asked. "Besides a whole lot of nothin'?"

Ashley O'Ballivan was in Stone Creek, and she was a whole lot of somethin', but Jack had neither the strength nor the inclination to explain. After the way he'd ducked out six months before, he didn't expect a welcome, knew he didn't deserve one. But Ashley, being Ashley, would take him in whatever her misgivings.

He had to get to Ashley; he'd be all right.

He closed his eyes, letting the fever swallow him.

There was no telling how much time had passed when he became aware of the chopper blades slowing overhead. Dimly, he saw the private ambulance waiting on the airfield outside of Stone Creek; it seemed that twilight had descended.

Jack sighed with relief. His clothes felt clammy against his flesh. His teeth began to chatter as two figures unloaded a gurney from the back of the ambulance and waited for the blades to stop.

"Great," Vince remarked, unsnapping his seat belt. "Those two look like volunteers, not real EMTs."

The chopper bounced sickeningly on its runners, and Vince, with a shake of his head, pushed open his door and jumped to the ground, head down.

Jack waited, wondering if he'd be able to stand on his own. After fumbling unsuccessfully with the buckle on his seat belt, he decided not.

When it was safe the EMTs approached, following Vince, who opened Jack's door.

His old friend Tanner Quinn stepped around Vince, his grin not quite reaching his eyes.

"You look like hell warmed over," he told Jack cheerfully.

"Since when are you an EMT?" Jack retorted.

Tanner reached in, wedged a shoulder under Jack's right arm and hauled him out of the chopper. His knees immediately buckled, and Vince stepped up, supporting him on the other side.

"In a place like Stone Creek," Tanner replied, "everybody helps out."

They reached the wheeled gurney, and Jack found himself on his back.

Tanner and the second man strapped him down, a process that brought back a few bad memories.

"Is there even a hospital in this place?" Vince asked irritably from somewhere in the night.

"There's a pretty good clinic over in Indian Rock," Tanner answered easily, "and it isn't far to Flagstaff." He paused to help his buddy hoist Jack and the gurney into the back of the ambulance. "You're in good hands, Jack. My wife is the best veterinarian in the state."

Jack laughed raggedly at that.

Vince muttered a curse.

Tanner climbed into the back beside him, perched on some kind of fold-down seat. The other man shut the doors.

"You in any pain?" Tanner said as his partner climbed into the driver's seat and started the engine.

"No." Jack looked up at his oldest and closest friend and wished he'd listened to Vince. Ever since he'd come down with the virus—a week after snatching a five-year-old girl back from her non-custodial parent, a small-time Colombian drug dealer—he hadn't been able to think about anyone or anything but Ashley. When he *could* think, anyway.

Now, in one of the first clearheaded moments he'd experienced since checking himself out of Bethesda the day before, he realized he might be making a major mistake. Not by facing Ashley—he owed her that much and a lot more. No, he could be putting her in danger, putting Tanner and his daughter and his pregnant wife in danger, too.

"I shouldn't have come here," he said, keeping his voice low.

Tanner shook his head, his jaw clamped down hard as though he was irritated by Jack's statement.

"This is where you belong," Tanner insisted. "If you'd had sense enough to know that six months ago, old buddy, when you bailed on Ashley without so much as a fare-thee-well, you wouldn't be in this mess."

Ashley. The name had run through his mind a million times in those six months, but hearing somebody say it out loud was like having a fist close around his insides and squeeze hard.

Jack couldn't speak.

Tanner didn't press for further conversation.

The ambulance bumped over country roads, finally hitting smooth blacktop.

"Here we are," Tanner said. "Ashley's place."

* * * * *

Will Jack be able to patch things up with Ashley,
or will his past put the woman he loves in harm's way?
Find out in
AT HOME IN STONE CREEK
by Linda Lael Miller.
Available November 2009 from
Silhouette Special Edition®

This November,
Silhouette Special Edition®
brings you

NEW YORK TIMES
BESTSELLING AUTHOR

LINDA LAEL
MILLER

At Home in
Stone Creek

Available in November
wherever books are sold.

REQUEST YOUR FREE BOOKS!

2 FREE NOVELS PLUS 2 FREE GIFTS!

Silhouette® Romantic

SUSPENSE

Sparked by Danger, Fueled by Passion!

YES! Please send me 2 FREE Silhouette® Romantic Suspense novels and my 2 FREE gifts (gifts are worth about $10). After receiving them, if I don't wish to receive any more books, I can return the shipping statement marked "cancel." If I don't cancel, I will receive 4 brand-new novels every month and be billed just $4.24 per book in the U.S. or $4.99 per book in Canada. That's a savings of at least 15% off the cover price! It's quite a bargain! Shipping and handling is just 50¢ per book*. I understand that accepting the 2 free books and gifts places me under no obligation to buy anything. I can always return a shipment and cancel at any time. Even if I never buy another book from Silhouette, the two free books and gifts are mine to keep forever.

240 SDN EYL4 340 SDN EYMG

Name
(PLEASE PRINT)

Address
Apt. #

City
State/Prov.
Zip/Postal Code

Signature (if under 18, a parent or guardian must sign)

Mail to the **Silhouette Reader Service:**
IN U.S.A.: P.O. Box 1867, Buffalo, NY 14240-1867
IN CANADA: P.O. Box 609, Fort Erie, Ontario L2A 5X3

Not valid to current subscribers of Silhouette Romantic Suspense books.

Want to try two free books from another line?
Call 1-800-873-8635 or visit www.morefreebooks.com.

* Terms and prices subject to change without notice. Prices do not include applicable taxes. Sales tax applicable in N.Y. Canadian residents will be charged applicable provincial taxes and GST. Offer not valid in Quebec. This offer is limited to one order per household. All orders subject to approval. Credit or debit balances in a customer's account(s) may be offset by any other outstanding balance owed by or to the customer. Please allow 4 to 6 weeks for delivery. Offer available while quantities last.

Your Privacy: Silhouette is committed to protecting your privacy. Our Privacy Policy is available online at www.eHarlequin.com or upon request from the Reader Service. From time to time we make our lists of customers available to reputable third parties who may have a product or service of interest to you. If you would prefer we not share your name and address, please check here. ☐

SRS09R

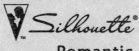

COMING NEXT MONTH

Available October 27, 2009

#1583 BLACKOUT AT CHRISTMAS
"Stranded with the Bridesmaid" by Beth Cornelison
"Santa Under Cover" by Sharron McClellan
"Kiss Me on Christmas" by Jennifer Morey
In these short stories, three couples find themselves stranded in a city-wide blackout during a Christmas Eve blizzard.

#1584 THE COWBODY'S SECRET TWINS—Carla Cassidy
Top Secret Deliveries
All Henry Randolf wants for Christmas is to be left alone. But Melissa Morgan shows up at his Texas ranch with adorable twin boys— quite clearly *his* twin boys—and he knows his life will never be the same. When a crazed killer puts the new family in his sights, Henry and Melissa must learn to work together—for their love and for the safety of their boys.

#1585 HIS WANTED WOMAN—Linda Turner
The O'Reilly Brothers
As a special agent, Patrick O'Reilly always has to put duty before desire. But his current suspect, Mackenzie Sloan, is tempting him beyond belief. Her eyes assert her innocence, though the evidence is against her. Will Patrick decide to trust his head…or his heart?

#1586 IMMINENT AFFAIR—Sheri WhiteFeather
Warrior Society
The first time warrior Daniel Deer Runner met Allie Whirlwind, he was injured saving her life. Now there are gaps in Daniel's memory— a memory that includes falling in love with Allie. But when Allie's in danger again, he's hell-bent on protecting her. Will their old feelings resurface before time runs out?

SRSCNMBPA1009